Whitetails
and
Tall Tales

ISBN-13: 978-0-9972920-9-1
ISBN-10: 0-9972920-9-1

Front cover design by Elizabeth K. Bramlett

First printing, September, 2017

See all books by Susan Lindsley at her website: yesterplace.com

Author's email: yesterplace@earthlink.net

Published by:

ThomasMax Publishing
P.O. Box 250054
Atlanta, GA 30325
thomasmax.com

Praise for *Whitetails and Tall Tales*

Lindsley's stories ring with the clarity of an October morning in the piney woods of the deep south. Their language cuts to the bone of what needs to be said: "Just go back to sleep, will ya," grumbles one half of the Midnight in the Marriage dialogue. Once you dive into Lindsley's stories, you'll likely not sleep until long after midnight, when you'll put the book down with a sigh of regret that you've finished it. – **Dana Wildsmith**, Educator, poet, author, *Back to Abnormal* and *Jumping*

These stories are very reminiscent of those I love so much written in a by-gone era when you couldn't wait to open the latest issue of *Field & Stream* or *Outdoor life* to glean what was inside. This book will no-doubt bring considerable enjoyment, and a few smug laughs, to hunters and non-hunters alike. I love Susan's "take-no-prisoners" style!"– **Duncan Dobie**, freelance outdoor writer, editor, photographer. Member Georgia Outdoor Writers, author of eight wildlife books and numerous hunting articles in regional and national magazines.

A woman of the fields, of the earth, and of the red Georgia clay, Susan shares her enthusiasm for hunting and fishing, and guides us into the woods. As she leads us into the world of wild turkeys, foxes, elk, and deer she reminds us of our God-given dominion over the beasts of the field, and the respect we must have for them. Her southern dialect filters through the good red earth and oozes poignancy onto the written page. – **Janet Sheppard Kelleher**, author of *Big C, little ta-ta: Kicking Breast Cancer's Butt in 7 Humorous Stories,* Amazon best seller.

A captivating collection of short stories is authored by an obviously experienced lover of the great outdoors! Good, enjoyable reading. – **Okefenokee Joe**, AKA **Dick Flood**, wildlife host, folk hero, songwriter, educator and Emmy Award winner.

Whitetails and Tall Tales

ThomasMax

Your Publisher
For The 21st Century

ACKNOWLEDGMENTS

I owe special thanks to those men and women who reviewed the manuscript and gave me so much support—Dana, Jan, Dobie, and Okefeenokee Joe. Thanks are also due Ben R. Baker for an email comment that gave me the idea for the story "Tilting Stone Mountain," and to Bill Vanderford for helping me with details in the story about the world record bass.

Thanks to my sister Thulia Bramlett and my school buddy Pat Blanks who helped me in my attempts to avoid the horrors of typos and misspellings. Any that remain are my doing, certainly not theirs.

My life partner Gail, as always, has listened to my ideas, read manuscripts and offered unconditional support.

Lee Clevenger and Preston Ward, my publishers, have endured my many changes of mind about this or that without complaint. Thanks guys.

For Janet Sheppard Kelleher

Friend, hunter, survivor, inspiration
and
author of the best-selling book:
*Big C, little ta-ta: Kicking Breast Cancer's
Butt in 7 Humorous Stories*

TABLE OF CONTENTS

THE DEER CAMP

Three alarms sounded at 4:30 a.m. Male voices grumbled and cursed. One said, "I ain't getting up this morning and don't either of you think you're going to my stand. I'm sleeping in and going out about nine."

"You sleep in, your stand is open for either one of us," came the reply.

"Billybob, don't you dare," Jimmy growled. He unzipped his sleeping bag and rose, bringing out with him the smell of old sweat and dirty male.

"I thought you were sleeping in," Billybob taunted. "If you are, at least stay in bed while we have breakfast."

"You ain't going to my stand," Jimmy repeated.

"Oh, shut up and go back to bed. Can't you take a joke? You're the one always picking on everybody else."

Jimmy stared at his brother for a long moment and then returned to his sleeping bag. While the other two men drank coffee and finished up the last few donuts, he began to snore.

Billybob whispered to Morgan, "I'm going to his stand."

Morgan whispered, "You do and kill something, he's likely to kill you. You know what kinda temper he has."

"Don't you tell and I won't. I got one-a my stands down the same road, just down the other fork. I'll say I got it there. He'll never know unless you tell."

Three hours later, the roar of the four-wheeler when Billybob returned to camp lured Jimmy outside. He was dressed for the hunt.

Across the back of the four-wheeler lay *the buck* Jimmy had captured several times on his trail camera. Always about 2:00 in the morning.

"You done killed my buck," he growled at Billybob.

"Naw, I didn't. He's anybody's buck if he shows himself to any-body. He ain't got your name pasted on him anywhere I could see."

"You done killed my buck. You knew I was going after him this morning."

"You didn't drag yourself out of that there sleeping bag. You don't hunt, you don't own no specific deer."

Billybob pulled a Bud from the cooler on the stoop, sat down on the top step and chug-a-lugged half the contents. "Boy, that tasted good. You gonna help me gut that critter?"

"No way. You kill 'em, you gut 'em. I'm going hunting." Jimmy gathered his gear, strapped a cushion to his belt and his green LL Bean gear bag/fanny pack around his waist. He stuck his Ruger into the gun rack on his Honda four-wheeler and cranked up.

With a wave at Billybob, he left for his stand.

He parked at the fork where his stand was some four hundred yards straight ahead and Billybob's down the trail to the right, near the creek. As he neared his stand, he saw yellow jackets buzzing and he knew. But to be sure, he followed them. They buzzed over blood. Lots of blood. Busy with a free meal, they ignored him.

"Damn him," Jimmy screamed to the morning. "He killed that deer here."

In spite of the three-week drought, the trail was easy to see, both the trail the deer had run as he died and the broken weeds and sticks where Billybob had pulled the carcass out of the woods and loaded it onto the four-wheeler.

He followed the yellow jackets another few yards into the woods and found where the buck bled out, blood clotted on the pine straw.

"I'll kill him," he muttered. "All my life, he's done this. Time I stood up to him."

Jimmy headed back to camp. His deer, the buck he had hunted all season, was dead. Billybob would soon be too.

He put his four-wheeler into high gear and ripped up the ground as he returned to camp. Morgan had returned and had obviously helped their brother field dress the deer. They both had half-washed blood on their forearms, but a beer in hand.

"Back already?" Billybob asked.

"I'm gonna kill you, you son of a bitch. You went to my stand. You killed that deer just to piss me off. And I'm gonna kill you."

Leaving the machine in gear and running, Jimmy jumped off the Honda. As it rumbled across the weeds, he didn't bother to watch it. Morgan hollered and ran after it, but it slammed into a tree. Morgan switched it off and turned around.

Jimmy held his gutting knife below his waist with the blade tip pointed up. Morgan gritted his teeth as he recognized the grip—go in low into the belly with the point up and rip upwards from below the ribs into the heart. He yelled, "Hey, Jimmy, don't do that!"

"You keep out of this, you hear? I told you both I'd kill you if you went to my stand. He didn't just go there, he killed my buck."

"That's no call to kill him. He's our brother."

"I don't care who he is. He killed my deer."

Billybob threw his half-finished beer at Jimmy and jumped off the end of the porch. Morgan pulled the Ruger off the gun rack on the four-wheeler. He hollered, "Jimmy?"

Silence for a moment. The click as Morgan pushed off the safety turned Jimmy's attention to him.

"You gonna shoot me with my own gun?"

"If you don't put down that knife, I might."

"You ain't got the guts."

Morgan fired one round. It hit the camphouse door.

"I could just nick your leg. Put an end to your hunting. Maybe forever if I mess it up just right and they have to cut it off. Now put down that knife."

Jimmy faced Morgan. The rifle did not tremble but remained steady and pointed downwards. Toward his legs.

He shifted the knife to his other hand and back again, this time gripping the tip of the blade. He raised it overhead and threw it at Morgan.

Morgan pulled up the rifle as he tried to dodge the knife.

The knife moved faster than Morgan and slammed into his chest. He rocked back as he pulled the trigger.

Billybob screamed. "Noooo."

His two brothers lay dead.

THE LADY AND THE COYOTES

She saw the coyotes through the kitchen window while she washed breakfast dishes. Five of them twisted around each other as they scavenged under the persimmon trees forty yards from her porch. *Fool fox hunters, bringing them here. They've done in the rabbits and everything else they can catch. Including that fawn last summer.* By the time she finished dishes, the coyotes were gone.

An hour later, the wind had gotten up, and she settled in the glider on her front porch where she could see the two persimmon trees. Even in daylight, some critters would come for the fruit the wind was putting down. The sun was too high for the pair of foxes to be out hunting, but with the rut in, who knew what deer might come by.

She didn't have a long wait.

A doe jumped the fence and trotted toward the persimmons, a buck behind her, his nose extended so that his antlers flanked his neck. His grunt of anticipation carried to the porch and then quieted as he pushed his nose into doe's rump. She minced forward and then stopped. He reared, mounted her, thrust once, and the mating was over.

He lifted his head and sunlight caught his antlers.

Oh, my gawd! That's him. The elk.

Ten days ago, the first time she had seen the whitetail buck, he was under the same persimmon tree, his head down as he sniffed out food. But when that head came up, his rack seemed to rise to the sky; the main beams curled outward beyond his ears and then upward. The beams were so thick she knew she couldn't reach her fingers around them at the base.

This buck made the monsters of her childhood seem small. At five years old, she had seen a buck brought from Michigan by a neighbor and that northern deer had stood larger than any she'd seen in her picture books, bigger even that Bambi's father.

The doe trotted into the thickets, the *elk* behind her.

I think I'll have a go at him. Time to get my life back. The leg's fine.

She rubbed her shin where the bone had protruded last hunting season when the deer stand had collapsed under her. The scar was still tender, but she no longer limped.

She made herself wait two hours and then squeezed a drop of Siberian pine oil on each of her hiking boots to cover the human scent and left the house to track the buck. His hoofs splayed from his weight even at a walk, and the trail was easy to follow—through the thickets, across the long meadow, along the pine ridge and though the hardwoods to the swamp.

When she reached the path that ran alongside the creek she stopped. Just ahead on her left stood the Osage orange tree. The stand was gone. Paul had removed it—the platform that had tilted when the support broke under her as she stepped onto it. Sight of the tree flared pain into the leg, the millisecond of the fall exploded in memory like a year of terror. She shivered.

Gotta get back on the horse or I'll never hunt again.

She stopped beside the tree and forced herself to look up at the site of the old stand. Paul had indeed removed all sign of it.

She turned back to the trail. Twenty yards farther along she found the elk's scrape line—a dozen pawed places where he had urinated to let an estrus doe know he was around. He had shredded the limbs hanging over the scrapes, and between scrapes, he had raked his antlers on trees, ripping bark off in long strips. Both the bare trees and the inside of the torn bark were bright yellow, and sap still ran from them.

"Fresh," she whispered.

Even if his doe of this morning was still in estrus and receptive tomorrow, he'd run this line again within three days. She picked out a pine thirty feet from the path that would give her a view at least fifty yards both ways down the path.

She returned home for her portable deer stand, a crescent wrench, slip-joint pliers and her pull-up rope.

By noon, she had bolted her two-part Warren & Sweat climbing stand on the pine. Remembering the hunter whose climbing stand had come apart and dropped him to his death, she snugged the wing nuts to the bolts with pliers and crescent wrench. She placed her haul-up rope on the seat and lifted it above eye level so the buck could not see the white plowline. *Unless he comes down the hill right to the stand.*

Back home, she called her neighbor two miles away. "Paul, I'm going hunting tomorrow."

"You are? It's about time you got back to the woods. The leg doing okay?"

"Yes, finally. I saw the elk again today and tracked him down to the swamp, near where—near that beaver pond. You help me if I get him?"

"You know I will. And I'll bring Buddy and the four-wheeler. You hear the coyotes lately?"

"Saw five this morning. And last night I heard three packs. One ran through my yard not long after sundown. Kinda scary with those yowls. One group sounded like they were at Turner's and the others could-a been going up your way."

"They were. I lost a cow, and they cleaned it to the bone last night."

"Oh, lawd, that's a big loss. They pull it down?"

"No. She died birthing a calf. It died too. It's part of running a dairy, I reckon. "

"They give me the shivers. I haven't heard of them attacking anyone other than that ranger, have you?"

"No. But I know what you mean. They're getting so plentiful they're wiping out their own food. I worry over my cattle. I'm going to hire a trapper. Get rid of some of them. Anyhow, just give me a call and we'll be there to help with your deer."

"Will do. I'll call from the stand on my cell phone."

Long before first light, she was up, dressed, fed, and on her way to the stand. Rather than follow yesterday's trail, she drove her Chevy pickup to the ridge road and left it about a half-mile from the climber. A cow path she had walked for more than fifty years, now kept open by the deer, angled down the hill to the swamp and beyond her stand.

She formed a loop in her haul-up rope, ran the line through the shoulder strap of her Ruger .44 magnum and over the end of the stock, and laid the rifle flat on the ground. She removed her fanny pack, ran the rope through the belt and knotted it. She looped the other end around her wrist and scrambled into the deer stand. With her feet strapped onto the foot rest, she climbed the tree: Stand up, pull up the seat, sit down, pull up the feet. With care, the only sounds she made sounded like a rutting buck horning a tree.

Twenty feet up, she stopped, buckled her safety belt, pulled up the rifle and fanny pack, hooked the fanny pack on one of the arms of the seat, and laid the rifle across her lap. She curled the rope on the foot rest, checked that the safety was on, loaded the clip into the rifle, and jacked a shell into the chamber.

The sky exploded above her with alarm-clucking and flapping

wings. More than twenty wild turkeys flew from their roost in panic and landed uphill in other pines.

Damnation! But at least first light was still a half-hour away. Surely the turkeys would go quiet again before they flew down at daylight.

The partial moon threw a sheen across the beaver pond to her right. Unless the buck came in grunting, she'd not hear him in the frost-wet leaves. The train blew as it approached the crossing a quarter-mile away, and coyotes sounded off. Then silence fell, so total she could hear her blood pulsing. If it were this quiet at daylight, she thought, she would be able to hear her shadow breathing.

The eastern trees darkened against the sunrise. A pair of geese honked their way to the beaver pond and splashed down. A heron squawked.

Up the ridge, the turkeys dropped from their emergency roost with soft clucks and worked their way, scratching, up the ridge, and within a half-hour were out of hearing.

She glanced at her watch—a little after 7:00. Yesterday, the buck and doe had been in her yard about this time. Since wild critters moved a bit later every day, if he was going to show, he'd be here within the next hour.

Movement to her left caught her attention, and she eased her head around to look. Only a squirrel, running silent over the damp leaves.

Moments later, a doe emerged from the thickets by the beaver pond and walked toward the stand. She stopped, lifted her head, cocked her ears forward, looked up the ridge, snorted and bolted back down the path. The buck charged down the ridge, nose extended.

She did not move her rifle. *No way I'll shoot him running.* She could smell his musk glands as he went by. She could only watch as both flags waved at her.

She gave the deer another two hours to come back before she unloaded her rifle and lowered it and her fanny pack to the ground. She dropped the rope and climbed down.

I'll see you tomorrow, big fella.

She was back in her stand the next morning and in four hours of sitting saw only a spike buck. He sniffed along the path and disappeared to her left.

The third day, she was again in her stand a half-hour before light. The eastern horizon barely silhouetted the trees when he grunted nearby. The wet leaves silenced his footsteps, and in the predawn light she could see only vague movement under the trees. He pawed one of the scrapes, grunted louder and thrashed the limb overhead. She heard the soft splash as his urine hit the ground. Only a shadow.

Too dark. Too dark.

She smelled his musk.

When her stomach demanded food and her bladder demanded to be emptied, she climbed down and looked over the scrapes before heading home. She stayed several feet away from each to prevent her human smell from contaminating them. Not just the one he'd visited while she listened, but all showed fresh activity. Droppings lay scattered in one, and two others showed fresh urine and pawing. Musk and urine still scented the air.

Musta been here earlier too.

The fourth day, coyotes trotted by, black ghostly shadows in the predawn. Her skin broke into goose bumps as they yelped and romped below her, their voices calling their hunger.

Back at her house at late morning, she called Paul.

"Any luck?" he asked.

"Just bad luck. The coyote pack came by today. And the buck's been coming by at night."

"You thought about hunting in the evening?"

"Yes, but they usually run scrapes in the mornings. I'll try one more morning before I switch to afternoons."

"I've got a cow in heat. Come on up and let me smudge your boots with 'cow-in-heat.' That'll pull him in. I used it last year and got my biggest buck ever."

"I never thought of that. I'll bring my boots up this afternoon."

And I'll have yucky stuff on the stand, but who cares.

Promised rain and a cold front came soon after noon and as it pushed through, it brought the wind. Dawn would be freezing.

Morning found her tired and the wind still up. When she turned off the alarm, she considered staying in, but with her boots doctored with cow estrus she dragged herself up, ate quickly and dressed for the cold.

She was almost asleep, elbows on her knees and head leaned forward onto her palms, when she heard him grunt. *Don't move don't move don't move.*

He sounded to her right, toward the Osage orange tree and the beaver pond. She eased her head around to look that direction.

The buck stood some thirty yards away, almost broadside, with his head turned to the pond, ears forward. Under the limbs of the Osage orange. The wind moved the limbs enough to dance their shadows across his back His attention was locked on a swimming beaver.

Okay, Mrs. Beaver, keep him looking at you.

She took off the safety by pressing one side while supporting the other to prevent the metallic click that spooked a deer more than a gunshot. With the safety off, she brought the rifle to her shoulder, as comfortable shooting from her left shoulder as from her right.

Her heart thumped; sweat flooded every pore and a chill ran through her body. Her hands trembled. The fever took her.

Not now. Gawd, not now. She clamped her teeth, pulled the rifle tight to her shoulder and leaned forward so that her right elbow pushed into her thigh.

She pulled her finger away from the trigger. *No, shooting won't jar the stand aloose. It can't. I got it on tight.*

The rifle steady, she looked into the scope, adjusted the rifle to see the entire vision circle, put the crosshairs on the buck's neck, sucked in a deep breath, held it, slid her finger onto the trigger and squeezed.

The buck dropped. She exhaled. A squirrel barked. A gobbler sounded off. Up the ridge behind her, a coyote yelped and another answered.

She kept the rifle pointed toward the buck, but he did not move. *Neck shot's always best. Dead before they hit the ground.*

Her body was not ready to climb down. Her buck fever raged. *I haven't had it like this since my first two year's hunting. Must be cause of where he stood. I gotta sit a minute.*

When her hands finally quite trembling, she unloaded her rifle, re-tied it and her fanny pack to the pull-up rope, lowered them to the ground and dropped the rope, which splashed white on the rifle, fanny pack and leaves.

She began to climb down—lift her heels to free the foot rest, move it down a couple of feet, then stand up and lower the seat. She had made three steps down when coyotes yelped only a few feet behind her.

Six coyotes loped toward her, noses to the ground, tracking the cow estrus trail she had laid down on her boots. When they spotted the deer, they ran to the fresh meat. One lifted his head and yowled his pleasure, and in the distance several answered.

Looking down at her rifle and fanny pack, she yelled her frustration. No gun, no cell phone, no nothing. The coyotes ignored her. She broke off a half-rotten limb and threw it in their direction, but its thunk onto the ground did not disturb them. They tore at the belly to get to the warm entrails. Gaunt bodies showed their hunger.

I gotta get that fanny pack and call Paul. Maybe they'll run as soon as I get down. If they're afraid of people.

She was only five feet from the ground when she heard something galloping in the hardwood leaves behind her. She looked over her shoulder. A large coyote stopped on her trail. At her eye level.

Oh my gawd! It's him.

The large male looked at her, his yellow eyes gleaming. One ear stood erect. His right one flopped. She had shot off half of it when he and his alpha female had come loping toward her as she lay on the ground with her broken leg.

He licked his lips and started toward her. He stared into her eyes.

Oh, gawd.

Her body shook. She could not meet his stare.

She jerked the seat up as she stood and had barely secured it when she pulled up her foot board. Each jerky step took her two feet up the tree.

Don't be scared. He'll smell you. Gawd, but I am scared. At least I'm up the tree. The ranger over in Jones County was on a four-wheeler when he got attacked by just one. I ain't about to get down till long after they've gone.

The wind swirled her fear scent. The coyote trotted to her pine.

Fifteen feet up, she settled herself and looked down to see him ignoring her, but with his nose sniffing her gear. He hiked his leg and urinated on fanny pack, rifle and rope.

Excited yelping uphill. Three more coyotes dashed into view and headed for the carcass.

The feasting male turned toward the new arrivals and growled, but rolled onto his back in submission to the approaching alpha male. The others yielded to hunger and ignored them. All pushed and shoved to get a place at the table.

She leaned her head onto her hands and against the pine. Her mind saw the destruction that she could not bear to watch. The sounds were bad enough.

She only killed a deer. The coyotes desecrated majesty.

Winner, Genre Fiction, Knoxville Writers Guild, 2015

THREE JUDGES

The threesome managed to wrangle an invitation to deer hunt last season and sat in assigned stands every Saturday for six weeks. None had shot a deer. None had even seen a deer to shoot. Fact is, they didn't know pea-turkey about deer hunting.

Last fall, they had gone together to the local sporting goods store to purchase rifles they knew nothing about. One of the trio was familiar with the name Remington—as a boy he had pounded on his mother's Remington typewriter. Another had seen Jimmy Stewart in *Winchester '73* and said maybe they should all buy Winchesters.

The salesman informed them that he personally preferred the Remington, so they all purchased a Remington 30.06. They asked about cartridges and he placed three boxes on the counter. Labels showed 150, 180 and 200.

"If I were you, I'd use the 150 grain. It flies flatter. And you want the Core-Lokt®. Or a hollow-point."

Each selected a box of the 150 grain Remington Core-Lokt®.

A good salesman, the clerk sold each a telescopic sight as costly as the rifles. For an additional small fee, he mounted and sighted the scopes for them, but warned they must go to the range and fire and adjust the scope as needed. He told them they needed a sling to make it easier and safer to carry through the woods to their stands. An extra clip would be a good idea, too.

"And you need ear protection when you go to the shooting range." He made another sale to each.

At the shooting range, the owner helped them make the final adjustments on the sights. When all three were hitting the target's bull's eye, he announced they were ready to go deer hunting.

Their host had great respect for the three. One was a federal judge, one ruled superior court in the county, and the third man passed sentence on small-time crooks, such as poachers. And the host had poacher problems.

So every Saturday of deer season, before daylight, he drove each judge to a deer stand, helped him get settled and safely raise the rifle to his stand. Four hours after light, the host returned. He hoped they did not ask to hunt the next year.

He need not have worried. That last day, over supper together with their wives, they decided, with a little female help, that deer hunting was not for them.

The next year, their former host was relieved to learn they had gotten interested in bird hunting. Since none had a bird dog, he feared they would ask him to take them quail hunting, but the one who sat in judgment on poachers got a lesson in duck hunting from the solicitor who prosecuted a duck poacher.

Yes, the prosecutor explained over lunch at the local lobster house, it was like deer hunting in that you get up before light. But for ducks, you put out decoys to make the duck think it's safe to land on the pond. You watch the sun come up over the water. It's not completely like deer hunting. Sure, you have to be still, but you can all sit together and call the ducks to you when they approach the pond. And yes, you can wear the same camouflage you used to hunt deer.

They agreed maybe duck hunting would bring them success. So as fall approached, they again ventured to the same store and purchased Remington .12 gauge shotguns. "No," the clerk told them, "you do not put telescopic sights on shotguns. If you bird hunt, however, you need to plug it to be legal."

"What do you mean, plug it?" the senior judge asked.

"Just put this short wooden rod in the magazine. That way, when a ranger checks you, he knows you can't load with more than the legal three shells. It's federal law, Judge." He grinned, paused and added, "I'll fix them all for you."

They shared the cost for a case of bird shot and asked the clerk where to go to practice shooting birds. He again referred them to the local shooting range and reminded them to take their ear protection with them. Off they went to the range.

They shot at clay pigeons all Saturday afternoon and returned the next day after church. They listened to and followed the advice "don't shoot at where the pigeon is but where it's going to be. That's how you'll get your ducks. Lead them just a bit."

With a dozen dead clay pigeons each, they ruled that it was time to go after ducks.

Miss Rachel, who owned a farm and had known each of these fellas when they were children and rode horseback out to her place to swim and chase tadpoles, said, "Sure, you can come duck hunting. There's a lot of them on my pond. And you don't need a retriever. The water's gotten shallow enough for waders."

"What are waders?" Jerry asked.

"Rubber boots and overalls all in one, so you can wade in the water and not get your clothes wet."

"Oops, I guess we go back to the store."

"Do you have a duck call?"

"No."

"Well, you better get one of those and practice. What about decoys? Do you have some of them?"

Back to the store they went. They asked the clerk what they needed by way of decoys, and he suggested several. They each selected three different ones. Each purchased waders and a call. They quacked in the store until the owner told them they could pass. He mostly just wanted them gone. Judges were not the best influence on hunters chatting about their actions in the woods or at the lakes.

Opening day, Saturday morning, Jerry drove his Escalade to pick up Mike and Don. On the way, they discussed cases of the past week. Mike as State Court judge had fined a deer hunter $300.00 for killing a doe out of season. Don, the federal judge, said he couldn't comment on the case he was sitting until it was over. Jerry said his most fun case had been at home rather than in the courthouse—some kid had tried to break into his car, set off the car alarm, and Jerry chased the boy down the street. He caught the kid and told him he was in real trouble. "I'm the victim and the witness. And I'm the superior court judge who can sentence you to life if I wanted to." He said he scared the kid so much he wet his britches, and would probably never get in trouble again.

At Miss Rachel's pond, they threw out their decoys. Some landed upside down, but who cared—they were in the water. The three sat along the bank. Miss Rachel kept it mowed and brush free. "Aren't we supposed to have a blind of some sort?" Jerry asked.

"Who cares? Aren't those ducks coming this way?"

The three judged that yep, here came their supper if they could just shoot right.

Don fired first and his duck began to spiral down. Jerry missed. Don fired again before Mike could, and down spiraled his second duck.

He whooped and shook his shotgun in the air. "I got two," he shouted.

He laid his weapon on the bank, splashed his way to the floating ducks and brought them both back to the bank.

"What kind are they?" Mike said. "They don't look at all like those greenheads I see when I'm fishing over at the big lake."

"I dunno," Don said. "What's the difference? They're ducks."

"Hey, look. Here come some more. Don, hold up and give us a chance."

Jerry and Mike brought down one each. "Now that's what I call a real duck," Mike said as he held up his greenhead.

They admired their kills and looked skyward for more victims. Don quacked his call when they saw ducks flying high in their direction.

"Hey, they're coming down," Don said. "This is my turn." The birds circled and as they came low and in range, Don fired. And fired again. Down came two ducks.

He brought them ashore and laid them by his first two. "Look, I got four alike."

Jerry asked, "You know, I hadn't figured we'd really get some ducks. Either of you know how to clean one or even cook one?"

"Hell, no," the other two proclaimed their judgment on the matter.

"Who's that coming?" Jerry asked and turned to the sound of a truck.

"Looks like Sergeant Phil," Jerry said. "He must need to talk to me. Might have a poaching case or something."

Wildlife Ranger Phil Eubanks stepped from his truck. "Hello, Your Honors. I heard the shooting and thought Miss Rachel had poachers, but she said no, it was you three trying to get a few ducks. Any luck?"

He strode over to them and looked down at the four ducks lying at Don's feet. "Who got these mergansers?" he asked.

Don said, "I did. I got all four of them. Didn't miss even once." He puffed out his chest with pride.

"Well, Judge, I hate to tell you, but the daily limit on mergansers is two. I have to give you a ticket and take your ducks. And I reckon we'll meet in Judge Jerry's court." He grinned, "And I reckon I might have to call Judge Mike here as a witness."

THE BLUEBIRD

She pulled her rolling suitcase and tried not to cry. She did not see the beauty of the park, the place she had come to with the child only a few days before the wreck killed both the girl and the father. If only he had put her in the child seat in the back, but no, he was too cocky about his own driving. He never thought a drunk driver would broadside them. He died and took his only child with him.

He left behind not only his childless widow but also Sarah, now an unemployed and homeless babysitter.

Sarah sighed and stopped beside a large oak, leaned her back on it, and stared skyward at nothing. A small hand took her empty one.

"Are you all right?" a voice asked.

Sarah looked down at a girl in a pink dress and Shirley Temple curls. A pair of brown eyes beneath furrowed brows looked up at her. "No, little one. I'm not all right."

"Well, I'm pre-cautious, so I can understand what's the matter if you want to talk about it."

"I lost a very dear friend. I am sad."

"Lost? Did your friend run away or did your friend go to see Jesus?"

Sarah had to smile. The child was indeed pre-cautious. "She had to go to see Jesus. And I miss her terribly."

The child frowned. "Well, then, maybe I can be your friend. I am real young and will live a long time and you won't have to see me go to Jesus."

Sarah laughed in spite of her sorrow. "I would like that. But where is your mother?"

"Oh, she's at home. I ran away."

"You what? You really mean you ran away from home?"

"Well, not exactly. I did run away from my sitter, though. She met up with some guy and they got to talking. She forgot she was supposed to be taking care of me. So I just walked off."

"That's not a smart thing to do. How old are you. Five?"

"Yes, but I'm a pre-cautious five. See my hands?"

She held them out toward Sarah and turned them over and back. "These hands are big for a five-year-old and I can play the piano. Even some Bee-toe-van. I'm going to be a great piano vir-ture-oh-so one day."

"I see. Well, let's go find your baby sitter."

"NO!" She stomped one foot and shook both fists up and down. Her face contorted into an angry frown and as suddenly returned to an expression of serene purity. "Let's walk over the park. I like that pink tree over there. What is it?"

"That's a cherry tree. What is your name?

"I'm LouAnn. What's yours?"

"I'm Sarah." She took LouAnn's hand as they walked toward the cherry tree. "Oh, look," Sarah said. "A bluebird. See?" She pointed to the nest box where the bird's head showed in the opening. The bird flew out and perched on the top of the box.

"The mama bird is feeding her babies."

"Can we feed them?"

"No, I don't think so. But maybe—" She released both the suitcase handle and LouAnn's hand. She slid a foot through the grass and when a grasshopper jumped, she caught it in midair.

She gripped it lightly by its legs between two fingers so that its body was above her fingers. She raised her hand toward the bluebird and the nest.

Nothing happened. Her arm began to tire. She was about to release the grasshopper when the bluebird flew down, seemed to pause in midair, grabbed the grasshopper from her fingers and flew back to the nest.

"Wow. Oh wow. I can't believe we fed the birds."

Sarah laughed with LouAnn. "I think she has become my bluebird of happiness."

LouAnn seized her hand. "Mine too. You are wonderful, Sarah. I love you."

Sarah squatted and hugged the child. "And I love you too."

LouAnn's cell phone rang. She looked at it and said, "Oh, it's my sitter trying to find me." She answered it and said, "This is LouAnn. I've been kidnapped by some mean old man and he says you have to pay a million dollars or he'll cut off one of my fingers so I can never play the piano again." She closed the phone.

Sarah scolded, "LouAnn! Let me have that phone. We've got to call her back."

LouAnn shook her head, stepped backwards away from Sarah, and kept the phone behind her back.

It rang again. LouAnn answered. "Alice, you are fired," she said and hung up again.

It rang again. LouAnn refused to answer. "It's just Alice. She's going to have to call Mama and I'll talk to Mama. You are going to be my new sitter. Let's catch another grasshopper for the bluebird of happiness."

"No, you call Alice back."

The child ignored Sarah and scrambled until she managed to catch a grasshopper. She almost squeezed it to death as she tried to pass it to Sarah. Sarah shook her head at the hopelessness of arguing with the child and took the offering for the bird.

When Sarah extended the snack upward, the bird hovered a moment before snatching the insect. LouAnn squealed with delight.

Her phone rang. "It's Mama." She answered it. "Mama, I fired Alice and I have the most wonderful person in all the world to sit with me. If you hire her, I can promise I'll never give you trouble again."

And so Sarah came to live with the Orleans family and the bond between the two grew stronger.

* * *

A year later, LouAnn insisted they go to the park. Her father drove and her mother sat in the front passenger seat, with LouAnn and Sarah in the back seat.

LouAnn was strapped in the child seat and in spite of the warmth of the spring day had insisted on several blankets which she formed into a tent over herself and the safety seat. She declared, "I'm an Indian in my tent and do not want to be bothered. I have my tomahawk and my bow and arrow and will fight to keep my tent."

Sarah proclaimed: "I am the general of all the Calvary and I have ordered my troops to remain in the fort for the duration of this peace treaty. No one will invade Indian Territory."

They reached the entrance to the park, only to find the gate closed. Sarah jumped out, "I'll check it, Mr. Orleans."

A small sign attached to the gate post read: *Park closed for the day for the first annual bicycle race.*

Back in the car, she explained and Mr. Orleans turned the car around and started home.

"I'm sorry, LouAnn. We can't get into the park today."

No reply from the Indian blanket tent.

"LouAnn?"

Still no reply.

Sarah pushed against the pile of blankets. No LouAnn. Only blankets and an empty safety seat.

"Oh my Lord. LouAnn's run off. She's not here."

Mr. Orleans slammed on the brakes. Mrs. Orleans swore under her breath and said, "Why the child promised. This time I'm just going to wear her out."

"I bet I know where she is. Back in the park."

"It's closed."

"Yes, but you know your daughter. Nothing is going to stop her once she makes up her mind. I know exactly where she has gone."

At the gate, Sarah leaped from the car. The gate was a gate, but no fence extended outside the limits of the road. Freedom for LouAnn to go where she pleased.

Sarah did not hesitate but took off at a run up the hill. Not at the first cherry tree, but beyond it, the third on along the ridge. Where they had fed the bluebird.

The child waved. Even from the distance, Sarah could see the wide smile.

"You little imp, you could have gotten me fired."

LouAnn pulled her hand from behind her back. "Mama wouldn't fire you. Here. This is for you so you won't forget me. Ever."

In her small hand sat a crystal bluebird of happiness.

THE JUDGE AND THE JURY

"George, you have to do this," senior judge William Conley insisted.

"We never hold a trial in that hick town. They don't even have a courthouse. Why this one? It's nothing but a moonshine case, a nothing case."

"The defense has asked for a local trial, and the prosecutor hasn't objected. You won't be gone but a day. Won't even have to stay overnight. It'll be a blast. When have you ever sat for a moonshine trial?"

"Billy, I'll probably hate you to my dying day, but I suppose I have to go."

"I'll get word that you'll be there Monday and ready to start by ten."

When George arrived in Jenkinsville, he found even less than he expected. With a population of less than three hundred, the town had one paved street and no traffic lights. He saw no signs of what might be a courthouse. He parked in front of Jenkins Store and entered. An elderly man sat behind the counter. George noticed the cash register—he had seen one like that in his youth almost fifty years ago. *I thought all those had gone to museums.*

"Morning," he said.

"Morning." The gentleman spoke around a dead pipe.

"Are you Mr. Jenkins?"

"That I be. What kin I do fer you?"

"I'm looking for your courthouse." He fingered quotes around the word *courthouse.*

Jenkins grinned and removed the pipe from his mouth. He poked at the cold ashes with a finger that bore evidence that it had been used earlier for the same duty. "It ain't a real courthouse. It's just next door, that old clapboard house. You looking for something special?"

"I'm here for the trial."

Jenkins leaned back, stuck the pipe between his teeth, hooked his hands into the straps of his overalls and spoke around the pipe. "Welcome to Jenkinsville. You the judge we been expecting?"

"Yes. Thanks. I'll go over to the courthouse." He strode out and down the street to the clapboard house. It needed paint—what was left from the last application was blistered and peeling. He walked up the steps and entered the long hall of a shotgun house. Stairs at the far end led to a second floor.

He ambled along the hallway and when he spotted a door marked "Clerk" he entered. Two ladies sat behind the counter at desks, each with a cup of coffee.

"Can I help ya?" one said. Neither rose.

"I'm Judge George Johnson. I'm here for the trial supposed to start today."

"Gosh, we are glad to see you, Judge. I'll let the lawyers know you're here. You want to go on up to the courtroom upstairs?"

He nodded. "Thank you. I need to get some things from my car."

The judge strode outside to his car, opened the trunk, removed the suitcase containing his robe and a briefcase with his copy of the indictment, returned to the courthouse and two-stepped up the stairs.

A man George figured to be about twenty greeted him at the top of the stairs. "Welcome, Judge. Let me show you where your office is at." The youth led him down the hall to a room with only a desk, a rotary telephone and a coat rack.

"Tell the attorneys I'll be ready to start on the dot of ten. I hope the witnesses are aware we are scheduled to start at ten today?"

"Oh, yes sir, Judge. Everybody's ready. They expected you here early and you got here plenty early. They be ready to start right at ten o'clock."

George looked at his watch. Ten minutes to spare. He nodded. "Thanks. You come get me when everybody is in the courtroom."

The youth nodded. "Yes, sir."

He came for George on the dot of ten and announced him to the courtroom. George entered to find the room packed. He sat behind the table that served as the bench and the trial began. George only half listened when the charges were read. He had studied his copy before he drove down. Everything seemed to flow. The *voir dire* went swiftly. Neither attorney objected to any of the potential jurors. The one witness strode to the witness chair, clad in full uniform of a state trooper. He took the oath and was questioned.

His testimony was brief: Smoke lured him to investigate and he found the defendant at the still collecting moonshine in plastic jugs as it ran from a condensing tube.

The defense attorney asked only two questions: "You sure it was whiskey?"

"Yes."

"Did you drink any of it to see if you got drunk?"

Everybody laughed. The trooper smiled. George rapped his gavel.

"No, I didn't have to drink it. I could smell it," the trooper said.

Testimony ended with the trooper. George thought the two attorneys were like peacocks or gobblers in mating season. They strutted around the room in turn. Each hooked his thumbs in his suspenders, studied the floor and the jurors and pontificated about guilt and innocence. The defending attorney insisted the trooper couldn't tell what was whiskey and what wasn't. The prosecutor swore up and down that anyone with good sense would know what whiskey smelled like.

George was relieved when he could charge the jury and they marched into seclusion.

He went to the office, removed his robe, leaned back in the chair, put his feet on the desk and closed his eyes. He'd take a nap while the jury tended to the conviction.

His nap lasted two hours. He woke to the tapping on the door. "Come in."

The young bailiff stuck his head in and said, "The jury can't decide. It's after five. Are you gonnna send them home or what?"

"They can't decide?"

"No, sir."

Dear God, I will absolutely kill William Conley when I get back to Atlanta.

"Send them home. Have them back here tomorrow at 9:00." He waved toward the door, but as the bailiff withdrew his head, George called, "Hold on a minute. Where's the best place to stay overnight?"

He got directions to the only nearby motel—about twelve miles out of town on the highway. He waited in the courthouse for everyone else to be gone and took his briefcase with him.

No pajamas. No toothbrush. No change of clothes. Just the word of William that he'd be there less than the day.

At least Jenkins Store, which carried everything from horse feed to toothbrushes, was not only next door, but was also still open. He bought supplies and went to the motel.

For two days the jury argued. At times, their voices rose enough for the bailiff in the hallway to hear them. Anger seemed to be directed at each other rather than toward the defendant.

George sat in the office with a Stuart Woods novel the first morning, but had to visit the store twice more for books. Nothing but used paperbacks, but at least some challenged the reader. It was fun to prop his feet up and forget the madness of the city and the city courtroom and to read *The Pelican Brief.* He even found two Miss Marple mysteries to tickle his thinking. But each night when he called home to report another delay, his wife complained that she would have to trash good food and when was he going to be home? Was he going to move in down there?

Afternoon of day three, the bailiff reported to the judge that the jury seemed to be in constant conflict, so George called the jury into the courtroom to poll them.

Six said guilty, six said not guilty.

"Why this disparity?"

The foreman replied, "This here what, Judge?"

"Disparity. Why this big difference? Do you think you can go back and agree on the defendant's guilt or innocence?"

"Ain't much chance, Judge, not with six of us being family and six of us not family."

"You were asked before being accepted on the jury if you were kin to the defendant. Which of you have lied?"

"Oh, Judge, ain't none of us lied. Ain't none of us kin to him. But some of us is family."

The judge sighed. *Now what? How in hell did I get sent here for this stupid trial? All over a liquor still.*

"Would you please explain how you can be family and not be kin?"

"Yessir, Judge. You see, my first cousin is married to a gal what is niece to his brother's wife's second cousin. That makes him family, only we ain't kin. Don'tcha see?"

The judge shook his head is disbelief. And wondered why he even bothered to ask the next juror who voted not guilty. "And how is he part of your family?"

"Oh, Judge, we are close family. My uncle's wife is first cousin to his wife's uncle. But we ain't kin."

"And you?"

The third man, still standing, hooked his fingers into the front straps of his overalls. "He married my wife's sister's husband's cousin. He be family but we ain't kin."

"And you?" the judge eyed the next man who seemed educated and was dressed in a business suit.

"He ain't no kin to me, and I don't rightly like to claim him to be family, but I got to since he up and married my sister in-law after he got her pregnant for the third time. We ain't got much use fer him, what with him making liquor and all."

The judge shook his head at the answer. "Making liquor? But you have voted him not guilty."

"Yessir, Judge. He's family. I don't claim him, but he is. I can't vote to send family to jail."

"But you just said he is guilty. "

"Yeah, Judge. But this here lawyer ain't proved it. I know he makes liquor. I buy it from him and sell it in my hotel up the road where you're staying, but that's what I know and you said to vote on what that man done proved. He ain't proved nothing. He ain't brought in no liquor for us to see and to taste and tell if it's what he made."

The judge looked at the prosecutor, who looked back at the judge and shrugged. The judge buried his face in his hands and tried to blank his mind. He couldn't. *Where did these good and true citizens come from? Why had the prosecutor not struck them for cause? Was there any way to send them back with orders to make a decision? Why bother? I know the chief judge must hate me. Otherwise why would I be here at the stupid trial.*

He looked back at the jury. One member still stood. "What about you? Are you part of his family too?"

"No, Judge. I ain't kin to him and he ain't my family, but I have to say he's not guilty cause Grant over here (he pointed to the hotel owner) owns the farm where I live and I got to vote the way he says or he'll put me out and I won't have no place to live and not any land to work."

"And he has told you that?" the judge asked.

"Naw, he ain't said nothing along them lines. He don't have to. You gotta live here, Judge, to know how life works. You stand by your family and you stand by your friends. All of us here know that. I don't know howcome you folks come here from the city and try to tell us how to live."

"I came here because the local judge admitted he is kin to the defendant and he recused so I was sent here to hear this trial. Now you men go back in the jury room and decide this case. You won't be going home until you agree, kin or family or not." He pounded his gavel.

The men rose, shook their heads, ambled out of the jury box and left the courtroom.

"Lord, deliver me," the judge whispered and left the bench.

Ten minutes later came a light tapping on his chamber door. *Oh God, don't let it be the Raven tapping on my chamber door. Let it be deliverance.* "Yes?"

"The jury just voted and agreed, your honor."

The judge breathed, *thank you God* as he shrugged into his robe and headed to the bench.

He called the jury in. The foreman announced their verdict, "Not guilty."

As was his custom the judge asked the jury members to stand for him to poll them. The first three said, "Not guilty, yer honor." The fourth man was a deacon in the local Primitive church, and George asked, "Did you vote not guilty?"

"Yes, I did, but he's guilty as sin. It got to where we had to vote not guilty or else."

"*Or else? Or else* what?"

He looked around the courtroom, turned to look at the juror next to him and turned back at the judge. "Just *or else*. If you lived here, you'd know what *or else* is." He sat down.

George surrendered. Family or kin or not. *Or else* or not. He was done. "Case dismissed." He banged his gavel, rose and left the courtroom. In fifteen minutes, he was in his BMW and on the road home, with dreams of what he might to do William Conley. Barbecue him? Just shoot him? Burn down his house? Better yet, find an attorney who is family but not kin to run against him for his seat next election.

THE TEENAGER AND THE POACHER

Deer season would open November 5, the day after her birthday. For the first time in her sixteen years, she would be able to hunt alone, without Father beside her in one of the platform or tower stands or in a climbing stand on the next tree.

For the first time, she could scout the land for herself, look for buck rubs on tree trunks, for scrapes under limbs along paths and Jeep roads. This year, she would get a buck she selected and not have Father say, "Shoot," whenever any buck, any size, walked into range.

She wanted a golly-whopper of her own. By herself. Except she would have to use Father's same shotgun she had used for the past four years.

Every weekend since Labor Day she roamed the family's three thousand acres, up one path and down another, across fields and into thickets, through the planted pines and the hardwood bottoms. She had come home some days covered with ticks and had to strip, shove her clothes into the washing machine and scrub herself with Octagon soap to remove the pesky pin-head-sized critters.

But a week ago she had found the perfect site. When she spotted the first tree oozing sap, she side-stepped from the trail. Ten feet off the path, she couldn't stay quiet but had to push and wiggle her way through the thickets. Bucks had rubbed numerous trees raw farther down the trail. Scrapes were scattered more than a hundred yards along the old cow path, with some overhead oak limbs thrashed bare.

As silent as she tried to be, she still spooked a deer. Saw only the white tail waving as the animal splashed across Soggy Bottom, where the spring never went dry and water overflowed the shallow banks. Water oaks, chestnuts oaks and white oaks dripped acorns. Persimmons dropped fruit. She spotted raccoon scat alongside deer droppings.

Got-a be a big one. Now where do I put up my climbing stand?

She surveyed the area for a tree with no low limbs. A sweetgum about thirty yards off the trail caught her attention. *I can get up that one a lot quieter than I can a pine. I'll need a hatchet to chop off those two limbs.*

To avoid walking down the hollow again, she cut to her right and went up the ridge. An hour later, she returned with her stand and supplies strapped onto her four-wheeler and parked half-way up the ridge on an old logging road.

She strapped a cushion and a holstered hatchet to her belt. She scattered her tools in various pockets of her cargo pants so they wouldn't rattle against each other. A thirty-foot-long cotton plowline lay over her neck and shoulder. The seat and foot rest of the climbing stand were strapped together with a webbed belt and their bars tightened down to prevent clanking noises.

She headed downhill with her load, staying on a cow path until near the bottom. She veered off to her right, into the opening between two rows of planted pines for the last hundred yards downhill.

After attaching her stand to the tree and snugging down all of the wing nuts with pliers, she climbed the tree to the first limbs, some twenty feet up. She removed the hatchet from its holster and chopped a limb off at four inches. The crotch would provide a leaning post for Father's shotgun.

She walked the stand back down the tree, lay the cotton plowline and a webbed belt on the seat and raised the seat up as high as she could reach.

Don't want a deer to see that plowline. She tugged on the back of the seat to be sure it was locked into the tree and would not fall no matter how strong the autumn wind became. She fastened the strap of the cushion to the backrest on the seat.

I'll have to dump a bunch of leaves off, but who cares? That buck won't know I'm here.

She shoved the pliers into a back pocket, tugged a camouflage handkerchief out of one cargo pocket and pulled the bottle of doe scent from the other thigh-level pocket. She splashed a few drops onto the handkerchief and dropped the cloth onto the closest scrape. With a half-rotted limb she moved the handkerchief around in the scrape. Satisfied she had scented the ground enough, she lifted the handkerchief with the stick and stepped carefully up the path a few feet to her left, shoved it into a bush and poked at it until it was jammed into the thick branches rising from the ground. The buck would smell it and thrash the bush but most likely not be able to dig out the handkerchief.

She almost danced uphill to the four-wheeler and went home. Now all she had to do was wait until November 5.

The days dragged for her—school and homework helped pass the time. Friday arrived, her birthday. She came home from school eager to finish her homework so the next two days could be spent in the woods. Getting up at 4:30 would mean getting to bed by nine. Not much time for homework.

But in her room, she had only opened her history book when her mother called her to supper.

We never eat this early.

But supper wasn't on the table. A box lay there—Remington in large letters. Two smaller square boxes flanked it. She whooped at the sight, the shout bringing Father into the dining room and a smile onto her mother's face.

"Oh, Father, you got me my own gun."

Father shook his head. "No, sweetheart. That came from your mother. I had nothing to do with making the decision. She knows how much you love to hunt."

She looked from Father to the box and then dashed to hug Mother.

"You'll have to get your dad to help you sight it in," she said. "The fellows at the store bore sighted the scope, but you'll have to do the final sighting yourself, they said. You two go to the store and use their range while I get supper ready."

At the store's rifle range she donned ear plugs. Her first shot was two inches to the left and an inch low. The store owner showed her how to click the adjustment knobs to change the sight line. Her fifth shot was dead center. "You're sighted in now for a hundred yards. Closer will shoot higher in the arc. Farther out, you'll need to shoot a bit higher."

She almost bounced with joy as she and Father returned to the family truck to head home.

"I can hardly wait for tomorrow. My own rifle. And I've picked my place to hunt and everything."

"You going to take your rattling antlers and deer call?"

"I sure am. I've figured out how to use the antlers up a tree, too."

At 4:30 when the alarm sounded, she jumped out of bed. She pressed her bare hand against the window, felt the cold, and dressed for frost. The smell of bacon lured her to the kitchen where both parents awaited her.

"You're on your own today," Father said. "Take your cell phone and call when you need me to come get your buck."

Before first light, she was out the door with rifle, flashlight and back pack containing her deer call and a pair of antlers. She took the four-wheeler along the ridge and kept it in low gear to not disturb the night with noise or the bottomland with exhaust. She parked where she had when she put up her stand. She took time to drop doe scent on her boots before setting off downhill.

The flashlight provided only a small circle for her feet to follow the path. She was almost half-way downhill when a deer blew across the hollow, on the next hillside. She cut the flashlight and listened. Nothing. Just a leaf floating by. A slight wind. Too early for the jays to be about and waking up the woods.

No, it can't see me. It's too far away. And can't hear me with the wind blowing leaves. It must be snorting at something else.

When she reached the stand, she clicked off the flashlight. The half-moon gave all the light she needed. She tied one end of the rope to the pack, ran it through the strap of the rifle and wrapped it around the stock to keep it from sliding against the backpack. The other end she knotted to the front bar of the stand's seat section.

She lowered the two sections to be able to step over the bars that hooked around the tree. She sat, stuck her boot toes into the leather loops on the foot rest, pulled the straps from behind her heels and tightened them down so the footrest would not fall off her feet.

Up she climbed, standing on the foot rest, pulling up the seat, sitting and pulling up the foot rest. Each set of movements took her up about three feet. When she was about twenty feet up and the rope was out of slack she stopped.

The limb stub was at shoulder level. Perfect for a rifle rest.

She pulled up her gear, laid the rifle across her knees, untied the backpack and let the rope fall by her feet. From the pack, she eased the two antlers and used the leather boot string to hold them apart, the string stretched across the arms of the seat. She removed the grunt call and stuck it into one of the thigh pockets of her camouflage cargo pants. From the other side pocket she removed the four-shot clip.

The webbed belt became her safety strap as she buckled it around her and the seat back. If she fell, the whole stand would go with her. She smiled. No way the stand was gonna fall.

She stood the 30.06 on her left knee and snapped in the clip. She grimaced at the noise, but had no choice; she slapped a cartridge into the chamber and let the bolt snap back. *Not gonna put another one in the clip. Too much noise. I don't need but one shot anyhow.*

With the butt of the rifle standing on the seat between her thighs, she leaned the end of the barrel against the junction of the trunk and the limb stub. It was rock steady. She would be able to use the antlers without disturbing the rifle.

She was ready. All she needed was daylight and the buck.

Night held on, and dawn seemed to be lost somewhere. Impatience gnawed at her but she reminded herself she was in the perfect spot to get a buck. Scrapes all around, and the area heavy with the odor of musk, the smell far stronger than last weekend. The buck had to have been staying in the area, probably looking for the "doe" from the scent she had laid down

As dawn finally began to lighten the area, she saw her own tracks where she had kicked frost, and a glance at her boots showed where the frost had landed. *It'll start to warm up by eight o'clock. Soon's the sun gets over the trees. Hope I've got him by then.*

The wind gusted. Leaves floated down, silenced by the frost. The morning stayed quiet.

A stick broke to her left. She reached for the rifle, but as her fingers closed on the stock, a man in camouflage came around the bend in the trail. No blaze orange. No business on the land.

Must-a come across the fence. But that's more'n two, three hundred yards. He had to crawl through the fence.

He carried a shotgun.

"Hey, Mista. Whatcha doing here?"

The man stopped, looked up, turned and trotted off.

"And don'tcha come back, you hear?"

Damn and double damn. He's probably run everything off for a mile.

She pulled her collar up and tried to scrunch deeper into her LL Bean down coat. *Maybe I ought-a wait another half-hour before trying to rattle in a buck. Let it go quiet after that idjit came in here.*

The sun rose, but she was too low in the hollow for it to reach her. Her toes began to tingle as they chilled. Shivering, she wrapped her arms across her chest and stuck her gloved hands under her armpits.

The sun tipped the top of a white oak on the ridge in front of her, across the wet-weather creek. *Time to talk to the deer.*

She pulled the deer call from her pocket and held it between her teeth. She lifted the antlers, closed her lips around the grunt call, and grunted twice. She clanked the antlers together and twisted them against each other for about fifteen seconds to create the sounds of two bucks fighting. She grunted again and dragged one of the antlers against the tree bark twice and slammed it into the brush of the limb hanging at her left shoulder.

Hoofbeats to her right. Hoofbeats approached from her left. She draped the antlers over the stand and lifted the rifle to her right shoulder. A doe came running from her left. Behind the doe trotted two bucks.

She had no interest in the spike, and the eight pointer was nowhere as big as the one she hunted.

The hoofbeats to her right stopped.

Over her right shoulder, she saw him. *The buck.* A dream monster. And off to the wrong side. She could only watch him. He lowered his head, shook his threat, grunted and stomped forward.

My gosh, he's gonna fight them over the doe. He thinks they were the ones fighting. I fooled all of them with my rattling.

The buck stopped almost directly in front her stand, lowered his head again, shook it to challenge and lifted it.

The spike fled.

The eight pointer shook his head to accept the challenge. The ten pointer charged.

Antlers clashed as the ten pointer locked his with those of the smaller eight pointer. They pushed, but the smaller buck lacked the weight and power of the older, heavier deer. The smaller deer yielded ground. The bigger deer broke contact and stood erect, but the smaller deer did not surrender. He began to circle to his right and the larger one lowered his head in anticipation of another shoving match. They clanked together, shoved and twisted heads.

She raised her rifle, looked beneath the scope to the iron sights, lined up on the bigger buck's neck and squeezed the trigger. He fell and did not move.

Dead. I got him.

The eight pointer fell with him, their antlers locked. He lay on the ground kicking and thrashing his neck, jerking the dead buck's head up and down.

She took a second shot and the eight pointer lay dead.

Two at one time. I can't believe it. I can't wait to get home. I gotta call Father to come help.

She searched her pockets and realized she didn't have her cell phone. She yanked the backpack around and felt in it. No phone. She cursed aloud.

She shoved the deer call back into her pocket, lowered the rifle, dropped the antlers and stepped the stand down as fast as she could manipulate the two parts. She patted each deer, whispered, "Thanks, big boy," to each.

She ran up the hill, the rifle bouncing against her back. She didn't bother to keep the four-wheeler quiet but roared home. Twenty minutes later, she and Father and Uncle drove the family four-wheel-drive Jeep down the hill between rows of pines.

Her stand no longer hung on the tree. It was strapped to the back of the stranger who stood over her deer. A tag fluttered from the antlers of each.

"Those are my deer, Mista," she shouted as she ran from the Jeep.

"Oh, no, Missy. They're mine. See? I already got them tagged."

"Yeah? Well, howcome my tags are in their mouths? And howcome my name's burned into the bottom of that stand you're trying to steal?"

She walked over, reached inside the larger buck's mouth and pulled out her tag.

"WOMEN AIN'T GOT GOOD SENSE"

Two days beyond my sixty-eighth birthday, I finally realized some law enforcement officers I dealt with believe women ain't got good sense.

They showed respect when I ran down a poacher in the woods or trailed a night hunter down the road while calling the ranger. Trial day always found me on the front row in the courtroom, perched behind the prosecutor, and when court was over the ranger and deputies would stop me in the hall to say thank you.

The local judge was a different matter. He held a grudge against me for years, since Mother filed against him for her cows he sold—and he took revenge whenever he could—like the time I caught a feller on my land, smoking gun in hand in the middle of deer season. Judge let 'im go 'cause, he said, he grew up nearby and knew my land lines and obviously I didn't. In other words: "You're a woman and you ain't got good sense."

Anyhow, my sudden view of reality started when I was sitting on my porch after sundown, having a rest after deer hunting all day. The rocker squeaked just right to make me want to doze a bit while Nate, who hunted several miles away, told me about the buck he saw that afternoon.

Then Nate said, "Somebody's lost."

I stopped rocking and listened. Somebody hollered across the road and just a bit to the south.

"Probably the man poaching on the Black Place," I said. "I heard somebody shoot over there this afternoon. A 30.06, the way it *kaboomed.*"

"I thought the land was leased," he said.

"It is, to a family of bow hunters."

We sat a few minutes and listened. The man whooped a few more times, but no one answered.

"I gotta go get some sleep if I'm gonna be in the woods afore light." Nate left for his camp across the county and I went to the phone to call my neighbor Paul.

Paul wasn't home. His wife answered and said he was helping look for Dr. Barron, who'd vanished. The fire department and some deputies with their bloodhound had come to help search, she said.

"That's who we heard hollering," I said. "I'll go up and tell 'em."

Well, I wonder why I bothered. When I got up to Dr. Barron's house, I saw the flashlights coming down the road from his fields, and I got out of the car. Mrs. Barron ran ahead of me to meet the searchers—three deputies (one holding a bloodhound on a leash), two fire-and-rescue men, a local wildlife ranger and some men I didn't know. Without Dr. Barron.

They found his car stuck in the mud down by his pond, but no sign of him or the car keys. Dr. Barron was already past eighty and wobbled when he walked. He also refused to use a cane. "It's for old folks," he always said.

"He's down south of here," I said. "I heard him holler down on the Black Place. Not half an hour ago."

"I've known him all my life. He'd never leave his own land," one of the strangers said.

"He would if he were lost," I replied.

"But there's a fence over there. He'd never cross it."

I drew a deep breath. "Yes, but the fence is down in places."

A deputy spoke up. "The dog's tired, and so are we. We'll have to look in the morning. We can't do anything else in the dark."

"He doesn't need to be out all night. Let's go down there with the dog. Didn't it take you that way?"

One of the deputies said, "It went in a circle. Dr. Barron wouldn't go on somebody else's place. Something happened to him. The dog must have picked up a coon or possum trail."

I exhaled sharply and rolled my eyes. "He wouldn't know where he was in the dark. He had to have gone that way. Besides, I thought the rescue dogs were trained to find people, not possums."

The stranger spoke up again. "We'll start over tomorrow. Who are you?"

I told him and asked who he was. Turned out he was a friend who used to quail hunt with Dr. Barron. Named Peter Robinson. Mrs. Barron had called him after she called the sheriff. He had obviously put himself in charge.

A few years ago, the K-9 deputies had used me as the escapee at my hunting site. They pulled the dog off my trail that day because they thought I would not have gone into the ditch instead of staying on the road. They put their own thinking ahead of the dog's nose then and now had done so again.

"We'll start out again in the morning," Robinson said. "You can help if you want to. Be here by eight."

"Okay," I said and shook my head. They just didn't believe *I* had good sense, and I knew *they* didn't. No use to say anything else. Maybe the old man would snug up against a log and stay out of the dew and frost. It was gonna be a cold night, and I sure didn't hanker to go looking by myself. I knew the old wagon roads on Black's land, but not his woods.

Be my luck to step in a stumphole, break my leg and be like the lady in the TV ad who hollers, "I've fallen and I can't get up." Nobody would know I was lost, so the deputies wouldn't come looking for me and I'd lie there till I died. I was too old to be off in the woods alone like that.

They loaded the dog in a truck, piled into their vehicles and drove off.

Next morning, I was at Dr. Barron's by eight and was surprised to see about a hundred men there, ready to search. No dog this time, however.

I was the only woman there except for Mrs. Barron and her maid, who were passing out coffee. Fear and exhaustion furrowed Miss Hetta's face. She met my eyes, nodded, mouthed a "thank you," and moved on with the coffee.

Robinson again put himself in charge of everything and told us to spread out and walk within five feet of each other and go over all of Dr. Barron's land.

"I told you last night, he's down yonder," I said and pointed south.

To no avail. Again Robinson insisted that Dr. Barron would never leave his own property.

I had to fight to keep from getting angry at these hardheaded, sot-in-their-own-ideas men who refused to listen to common sense. After I stomped over Dr. Barron's land for a couple of hours, I finally got the wildlife ranger to listen a bit and he allowed some of us should go check out Black's Place. But, I couldn't be the leader. Another stranger, another man, who didn't even know Dr. Barron, was put in charge.

We went to the fence, where only scattered oak and cedar posts remained. In a line some hundred yards long, with our backs to Dr. Barron's land, we moved south.

In less than two hundred yards we reached the east-west logging road, and our assigned leader insisted we go no farther.

"He'd never cross this road."

"In the dark, he couldn't even *know* it was a road. Or he might think it was one of his roads. His land is covered with roads. We need to keep going. Where I heard him last night he sounded a lot farther south."

"No, it couldn't have been him," our leader insisted.

He told everybody to go back, and I cursed him, but like an idiot I followed.

If I'd had good sense I'd have just gone on south and found Dr. Barron. In the daylight, I won't be likely to step in a stumphole in spite of the honeysuckle, other vines and logging trash all over the ground.

When we returned to the house, sandwiches and drinks awaited us, and we sat on the ground to eat.

Robinson surprised me. He sat beside me and asked what did I think might have happened.

I nodded to the south. "He's down yonderway. On Black's Place."

But Robinson shook his head. "He's as likely to have been picked up by a space ship as he would to be down that way."

A truck drove up. The driver hunted Black's land and supposedly only bow-hunted. I figured he was the one I heard shoot last night.

He got out of his truck and walked over to where Robinson and I were sitting.

"I hear Dr. Barron is lost," he said. "I was down this way last night and heard somebody yelling off south of here, down on the Black Place. It sounded like somebody lost."

Robinson scrambled to his feet and yelled. "Let's go, everybody. He's down on Black's Place."

Sure enough, we found Dr. Barron right where I had said. But then, men listen only to men because women ain't got good sense.

If I'd-a had good sense, I'd have just gone on after Dr. Barron by myself last night, stumphole or not.

Or maybe I did have good sense—if I'd gone out there in the dark last night and stomped my foot into a stumphole, I might've laid out there the rest of my three-day life, flat on my belly, my busted up leg stuck in the ground and the coyotes and buzzards circling as they waited to make a meal of me.

Honorable Mention: The G. T. Youngblood Short Fiction award, Southeastern Writers Association, 2012

JUNIOR AND THE TROPHY BASS

Junior could be found any afternoon leaning against his favorite oak beside the river, a jug of hooch at his right elbow and a cane fishing pole stuck in the ground by his left arm. Summers, he wore overalls without a shirt and didn't bother with shoes. On hot summer afternoons, he dangled his bare feet into the shallows.

Most locals smiled and shook their heads as they passed him by and thought *like father like son.* They gossiped to each other that Senior had killed himself with drink. Junior was headed the same way.

Others snickered, but the mayor plotted.

He had caught a massive saltwater bass on a fishing trip and planned to mount the thirty-pounder to hang on the wall until Mrs. Mayor said she wasn't going to have any dead fish hanging in her house. The trophy, hauled home intact and frozen, resided in a freezer ten miles away, in Tickleboro's grocery. The store owner called him twice a week get the fish out and to the taxidermist, but with the choice of the fish or his wife, he had chosen the wife—after all, she could cook up a good mess of fish when she brought it from the grocery already filleted.

This spring, Junior provided a perfect way to dispose of the fish.

He told Ripper what to do and sent him to Tickleboro for the fish. Ripper parked his rust-and-faded-blue Ford in front of the store and entered.

The vehicle's lack of a tag caught a passing deputy's attention. He stopped and stepped out of his Crown Vic. His badge proclaimed him to be Deputy Hicks.

Passersby slowed their vehicles to check out the cop and the truck he studied as he circled it. He looked in the driver's open window and saw two empty beer bottles, four full ones in a six-pack holder and a wedge of chewing tobacco on the seat. A shotgun and a rifle lay in a rack attached to the inside of the cab and blocking the rear window. He was staring in the truck bed when Ripper ditty-bopped from the store with the large package that smelled fishy.

"This here your truck?" Deputy Hicks asked.

"Sure enough," Ripper said and dropped his package into the bed where it clunked down beside one of several bags of corn.

"What's all that corn for? You got pigs?"

"Oh, no. It's most turkey season. I got to fatten them up afore I shoot me one."

"You not gonna shoot one while it's eating that corn, are you? Maybe I ought to tell the ranger you're bait hunting."

Ripper grinned. "Course not. I'll shoot him after he eats it good for about a week. Get some of that wild taste out-a him."

The deputy nodded toward the cab. "You're not drinking and driving are you? You got two empty beer cans here and the rest of the six-pack sitting right by you." The deputy wrinkled his nose. "I'm smelling beer on you anyhow. "

"Oh, I'm not drinking. I spilled some on me afore I left home. Look, I got to get on the road. That there fish is gonna start stinking when it thaws out. I got to get it to the river over in Stevensboro."

"To the river? That fish is dead and frozen. You planning to put it in the river? There's no alligators this far from the swamps."

"Oh, I'm not after an alligator. Mayor Stevens, he's after Junior."

"Junior? You mean that drunk?"

Ripper grinned. "Yeah. Mayor Stevens and me and some friends, we gonna fix him good with that fish."

The deputy grinned. "What's the plan?"

"I'm sorry, Deputy Hicks, but I jest can't tell. But I tell you what. I'll come back up here tomorrow and let you know how it goes. We jest can't chance on the word getting to him about what we gonna do."

"A-right. Go on. Be back tomorrow and let me know. Catch me at the jail. Okay? And watch how you shoot those birds."

"You betcha." Ripper scrambled into the cab, cracked open a beer can, shoved it between his thighs, cranked the truck and headed back to where Junior lay dosing on the river bank. He managed to consume two more beers by the time he got back to Stevensville and the truck made tracks on the road shoulder several times.

Two buddies waited for him in the shade of an elm tree about thirty feet away from Junior. He squealed to a stop and laid a few yards of rubber on the road.

"You drunk again?" Mervin asked.

"Yeah, but I got the fish," Ripper replied and pointed to the truck bed.

"Okay. Now who's going in the river?"

"I am," Buddy said. "Can't neither of you swim worth shucks."

Ripper reached into the truck bed and dragged the packaged fish to the tail gate. He unwrapped it.

"That there's the biggest damn bass I ever seen," Buddy said. "Where in hell did he catch that thing?"

Ripper shrugged. "I got no idea. Mayor Henry said he caught it on vacation."

"Reckon he might take us next time he goes up there?"

"Hah, he ain't about to take us. Not even if we vote ten times for him." Mervin said. "Let's get this here fish in the river."

They walked to the river's edge. Buddy sat, pulled off his brogans and socks, took off his shirt and kicked off his overalls to reveal purple and white stripped boxer shorts. "You best not be taking them shorts off," Mervin said.

"Y'all jest hold your horses," Buddy said and stepped into the river. He swam out a few yards and reached for the cork float on Junior's line. He slid his hand down along the line until he reached the lead weight and hook. He kicked back to the bank. With the others holding onto the fish, which was getting slippery as it thawed, he shoved the hook into its mouth and snagged it firmly into its jaw. Back into the river he lay on his back with the fish on his belly and kicked his way out some twenty feet and dropped the fish into the river.

He returned to the bank, used his shirt to dry off, put it on, and pulled his overalls back on. Although his feet were still damp, he put on his socks.

"You gonna get trench foot, putting them socks on wet feet," Mervin said.

"Be worth it when Junior wakes up and pulls in that fish."

"How long you reckon we got-a wait for it to thaw out?"

"It don't matter. Junior's so drunk he won't even notice it's frozen." Mervin went to the bank and jiggled Junior's cane pole.

Junior kept on snoring. He jiggled it harder. Junior did not wake up.

"Hey, Junior." Mervin shook his shoulder.

"Huh? Whatzat?"

"Quick! Set the hook. You got a bite."

Junior struggled to sit up, grabbed the pole and gave it a jerk. It tightened as the current pulled the fish downstream.

"By God I got me a fish!" Junior shouted.

He pushed himself up with one hand while holding the pole in the other. "It's a big one. It sure is pulling."

A passing couple stopped and looked. Mayor Henry came from his office to watch. When townsfolk realized something was going on, they gathered to join the excitement.

Junior backed up and shortened his grip on the pole until he was holding it near the end. The river continued to pull the dead weight downstream.

Junior backed up until he stumbled over the street curb and almost fell. He reached beyond the end of the pole, grabbed the line and walked his hands down it to the river bank. The fish's head showed in the shallows.

"My God, boys! Look at what I got here."

He splashed into the water and tried to grab the fish. It slipped away in the current. He grabbed again and managed to stick his fingers into the open mouth and seize the lower jaw. He lifted it one-handed, swung it over the water and threw it flying onto the bank. He leaped after it and straddled the dead fish.

"I done got me enough fish to last me a week, boys."

The trio of jokesters laughed with him. "That sure is one big bass, Junior. What bait you use?" Mervin asked.

"I don't recollect. If I can remember, I'm gonna use it again. I'm going home to fry me up some supper. You boys want-a join me?"

"Naw. It's your fish. You ought-a not be sharing it."

Mayor Henry stepped from the crowd. "Congratulations, Junior. That's the biggest bass I ever did see come from our river. Maybe you'll have to quit fishing now that you caught the best. You reckon it weighs twenty pounds?"

Junior smiled and showed a gap where he lost a tooth in a bar fight four years ago. He said, "Yessir, Mayor. It's at least twenty pounds. I'll be back to catch me another one just as soon as I finish eating this here one. There's got-a be some more like it in there."

A camera clicked. And another. Someone yelled, "Mayor, stand over by Junior."

Politician that he was, the mayor posed with Junior and the fish Junior held like a baby in his arms.

"I got-a go fix my fish," Junior yelled at the crowd. He left for home with his trophy firmly wrapped in both arms.

The crowd dispersed. The mayor returned to his office with dread that now Junior would be forever on the river, drunk and hoping for another fish. The trio joined in a three-way hug and danced to their laughter until they gave out of breath. They headed to the bar to celebrate.

The next day, word about town was that Junior had caught the world's record largemouth bass in the river and had taken it home to eat. Pictures of Junior, his snaggled-tooth grin and his fish appeared on Facebook, Twitter and You Tube. Someone managed to get pictures into the Atlanta papers.

Fishermen flocked to town and crowded the river banks. Boats appeared from upstream and downstream. The hamburger shop could not keep up with orders. The small convenience store and the local grocery sold out of soft drinks, bottled water, snacks, canned meat, bread and toilet paper.

The fourth day, the state game and fish biologist heard about the story in the papers and headed to town with a wildlife ranger driving his law enforcement truck with lights flashing and siren blaring. They went directly to the mayor's office.

"We have to measure the fish for the records. It'll put Georgia on the world map, a bass that big."

"Junior left here saying he was going to eat it."

The two state officials looked at each other in horror. They got directions to Junior's home, but as they walked out with the mayor, he said, "He's over there fishing again."

They had to push through the crowd watching Junior. He had his jug by his side and a line in the water. He lay propped against the oak and snored.

Ripper woke him. "Junior, you got company. Wake up."

Junior cranked out one more snore and sat up. "What's going on, Ripper?"

"You got company. Wake up."

The biologist came forward. "Junior, I'm David Scott, state fish biologist. I need to see that fish you caught. I heard it's probably not just a state record but may be a national record large mouth bass."

Junior laughed. "I ate that fish. Finished him up for breakfast. It sure was the best bass I ever had. My cat liked it too. I had to give it some seeing as how I don't usually feed it and everybody says it kills birds."

"You ate it?"

"Sure did." He grinned and patted his belly. "I ain't et that good in a heck of a long time."

"Do you still have any of it? Maybe the backbone? The head? We can estimate its size if we can get its head."

"I reckon the head's maybe still in the garbage can if you want-a go looking. I ain't one to poke around in the garbage. Ripper, show 'im whereat my place is and let him look in the garbage, but make him put it all back and close up the can. Can you? I want to keep on fishing."

Ripper and the biologist left. Junior took another snort of whiskey and lay back down. He was asleep before the investigators reached his home.

They dumped the garbage. There was the fish head.

The biologist swore. "How in hell did he catch that in a Georgia river? That's not a Georgia bass, it's a stripped saltwater bass."

Ripper snickered.

Stevensville returned to normal. Junior continued to fish. Alone.

THE LOGGING CREW

Four-thirty Saturday morning. She clicked off the alarm and threw off the covers. The small space heater had been unable to hold off the cold and she shivered while pulling on her hunting clothes. It would be a perfect day for her stand in the Honeysuckle Ridge pine.

Breakfast over, she headed down the highway in her rattletrap Jeep. At the gate, she turned into the pasture driveway. The gate stood open.

Stupid loggers. They know they are supposed to keep it locked when they aren't in here. She drove through and left the gate open. *I'll lock it when I come out. Nobody'll poach when they see the gate open.*

She drove into the woods and parked in the edge of the hayfield. Moonlight would be enough to guide her to the stand so she did not bother to pull the flash from her fanny pack. With her .12 gauge Remington in her right hand, she strode through the blue moonshadows along the trail through the tall pines. No wind stirred. The morning air would move upward, not outward, so her scent would not spread from the ridge-top stand but drift upward with the warming air.

She reached the broken pine limb she used as a marker to turn to the right, to the stand. She turned, walked twenty paces and halted.

Where the heck is the stand? It should be right here. She turned around. Moonlight showed only naked pine trunks.

No leaning ladder with a hood. She pulled out her flash and turned its beam onto the tree where she was sure the stand should be.

Ropes dangled and light glittered from the chain she used to lock the stand to the tree.

Damn. It has to be the timber cutters.

She turned back to the trail and headed for the stand off the ridge to her left. She no longer tried to be stealthy, but struck out at a hard fast pace. Daylight would be on her before she reached the other stand.

There, she found the ropes and chain dangling.

She sat against a pine while anger rolled through her. *Two stands gone. Both in sight of the logging road. I pulled the ones in the area of marked timber, but these two weren't in their way. Nobody but the loggers have been in here. One of them got the stands.*

Not the crew boss. He has a key to the gate. And he doesn't hunt.

So some of the men. Probably to sell the stands to buy whiskey. Even if I go to the home of all four of the cutters, the stands won't be there.

She moved her right leg to ease the cramp in her calf, and a deer blew off to her left. No need to even turn her head, but she did anyway and saw only a flag waving at her. The hooves were silent in the damp pine straw.

She went home and plotted.

On Friday morning, while the loggers were working, she placed another stand on Honeysuckle Ridge, same tree. She hung the same type of camouflage rack and added the same camouflage hood, but this one was longer, designed for another type of stand. It fell three feet below where she would rest her boots on the second step from the top.

Late that afternoon, she settled in the stand before the loggers left for the day and weekend. She was invisible and threw no silhouette against the thick heavy-duty material.

The pickup approached as the loggers headed home. It slowed, stopped. Their voices carried the twenty yards to her.

"Hey, look. Let's get back after dark. Get another one."

"Hush up, man. She might be in there."

"Naw, she ain't anywhere around. 'Sides, when I went out with the last load I seen her Jeep down the road off the other way. Been too much in and out here for her to be hunting up here till over the weekend."

Thank goodness I drove it a-ways down the road toward the soggy hollow off to the south instead of leaving it in the meadow.

She got comfortable for a long wait. Her safety belt gave her security enough that she dozed when darkness wrapped around the ridge. The town's lights kept the eastern sky bright. The moon would be awhile rising, and when she pulled the camouflage back from her peep holes, she could see stars. *It's been a long time since I watched the evening stars.*

Time seemed to sleep. But the night did not. Something rustled the leaves as it trotted to her. She peeked. A shadow moving through the shadows.

Coyote. Too big for a fox.

She sat through a long silence. A smell came with slight sounds of movement. *Skunk.* She tried to spot it through one of the windows and finally managed to see the white stripe.

A truck. Here they come.

It stopped on the logging road. Two doors opened. Two voices. Footsteps approached.

"You cut the chain. I'll get the ropes."

"Okay."

As they men stopped by the tree, she cranked a shell into the chamber of her .12 gauge and voiced a deep-throated laughter. The laughter of a ghost or demon or *The Shadow* of long-ago radio.

"Run," one said.

She slid down from the stand and repeated the laughter.

They were already climbing into the truck. The driver gunned it off. They would have to go to the logging yard to turn around.

She pulled out her cell phone and dialed 911, asked for the sheriff. When she reached the dispatcher, she said, "Carolyn, they're back. Please send a couple of guys out to the gate as we planned."

She heard Carolyn call to a deputy and the sound of footsteps trotting on the tile floor in the office.

"They're on the way," Carolyn said. She laughed. "Did you crank that shotgun like you said?"

"I did. They've driven back into the woods. I'm headed to my Jeep and will meet the deputies in the field inside."

The deputies arrived in two patrol cars as she drove her Jeep into the field.

They pulled all three vehicles into the shadows along the edge and waited for the loggers. Two hours later, they heard the rumble of the pickup as it eased into the meadow.

The deputies cranked up their vehicles, and with lights flashing and sirens blaring, they blocked the truck.

She trotted up to the three vehicles as the two loggers got out of their truck with their hands up.

The deputies approached.

One of the loggers said, "Deputy Willis, what the hell you doing here? Your brother asked me to get him a deer stand."

THE GUIDE AND THE ELK HUNTER

For five days, they slogged through snow and camped in the cold. Bert cooked meals and led the idiot to several excellent elk. But the hunter said "No," to each one. "It's not big enough. I want one that has a rack so tall I can hang it in my trophy room and his nose will touch the floor and his antlers will rake the ceiling."

Anybody would take any of the elk we've seen, Bert thought.

On the morning of day six, they woke to more falling snow. Bert faced the blizzard to feed the three horses, glad he had left them on the south side of the timber hedgerow last night. As it was they stood facing south, hunched against the wind. He pulled the tarp aside and found the saddle blankets, which he laid over the horses. The feed was low. They would have four more days to hunt and then he would guide the hunter back to the airport and be rid of him.

The sorry S. O. B. is gonna sleep in till the storm is over. No way I'll be cooking today. He can eat jerky and I'll melt snow for water.

The storm passed through by mid-afternoon, and Bert left the hunter in camp to scout over the ridge. *Maybe I can find something today and be rid of him tomorrow*

The scouting trip up the ridge gained him only tired legs. The elk had retreated into the timber with the added snow.

Two days later, the temperature had climbed enough above freezing for the elk to move into the open. Bert thought of the warm up as Indian Summer—that time in winter that in the old days the Indians would have found it warm enough to hunt game or white folks. Right now, he had to find an elk. A big elk.

Bert glassed the valley below and the ridge across the valley. Half-way up the next ridge he spotted an elk big enough for his own dreams. Even the idiot said, "Yep, that one looks about right."

Bert led the idiot in a two-hour hike around the arm of the ridge, across the valley and up to the tip of the other ridge. He left the hunter behind the lip of the ridge and scanned the area for the elk. It browsed about two hundred yards below and to the right. The wind drifted from the elk to them.

Should be an easy shot, if the idiot is the kind of a shooter he claims to be.

He signaled the hunter to ease up. "Lie flat. You'll have a good shot if you just wrap your sling and prop on your elbow. You can't miss if you're as good as you tell me."

"Sure. And yep, I'm as good as I say. I never miss my target."

He followed Bert's advice, lay down and aimed. He fired. The elk fell.

The elk thrashed as they approached. *Idiot shot off the front legs. How in hell did he do that if he never misses?*

"Put it out of his misery," Bert ordered.

The elk lunged and threw himself forward with his back legs. The hunter laughed and shot one of back legs. The bullet raked the other leg and blood surged from a vein.

"Damn you," Bert shouted. "Kill that poor animal."

"In a minute." The hunter pulled out his cell phone and ordered Bert, "Take my picture."

Bert took the phone without removing his gloves.

The hunter walked up to the elk, laid his rifle against the body and got on the other side.

"Dispatch the elk," Bert said again. *Idiot. Putting the rifle so it points to himself and not having enough sense put the safety on.*

"No. I like my pictures without the animal's tongue hanging out. That way, all the other hunters know I posed with it alive."

Bert approached with the cell phone in one hand and snapped several pictures as he closed the distance. He half stumbled, reached toward the leaning rifle as if to catch himself and pulled the trigger.

"Oops," he said, "the elk kicked the rifle." He erased all of the pictures except the first one.

He left the rifle leaning against the elk's belly and used his own rifle to dispatch the elk. He called the ranger station on the hunter's satellite cell phone to report the weird accident and to ask for help in moving the body.

Instead of waiting, he field dressed the elk. He would pack it out on the horses and take it to a family in need. Idiot would fly home in a box.

THE OLD WOMAN AND THE TURKEY

Four in the morning and she lay awake, waiting for the alarm. Opening day of turkey season. Her first hunt since Billy died four days after their sixty-second wedding anniversary. *Gawd, how I miss him. Just one more hunt.* She longed to watch spring spread itself out before her, to hear the day awaken and the toms gobble from the pine ridge.

One more hunt to show that no-account son she didn't need to go to a nursing home.

Eighty-one ain't too old. You're not old until you forget and can't remember you've forgotten. I still can remember things even when I do forget something for a little bit. Folks under sixty don't know about getting old. Old is only thinking old.

Besides, I gotta get that bird afore noon if I'll make that whoop-de-do. And I gotta be there to get my deed.

She smiled. Today she'd get the deed to the land the railroad took from her mother's family more than a hundred years ago. And she'd put an end to her son's talk of a nursing home. *He'll see I can live alone when I outsmart and kill Buster. I'll show that boy. All he wants anyhow is everything I got, all me and Billy worked for.*

That gobbler had to weigh over thirty pounds—he was so tall he could eat off the hood of her Subaru Outback. And so slick he'd outwitted hunters for four years. She reckoned if turkeys could laugh, Old Buster laughed loud and long.

She reached out, switched on her bedside lamp and turned off the alarm although it was only half-past four. She had plenty of time for breakfast. Even time to waste before light.

For a moment she sat on the edge of her bed and let herself drift back to the river swamps with her father. Half Cherokee, he taught her about turkeys and how to call them. He made her a cedar box call when she was only seven, and she had used it until she'd worn the edge down. She had tried to copy his voice calls, but he told her she didn't have enough Indian in her to wrap her voice around the words of a turkey. He said she had to stick with her cedar box. Still, she had continued to practice soft yelps without the aid of a man-made mouth call but had to agree with her papa.

She had stuck to the cedar box Billy had crafted for her the year they married. *Oh, Billy. I do miss you.* Her mind flashed to the morning she and Billy walked home from their first hunt of that last season, the day he was toting her turkey home and fell dead between the rails with a heart attack.

I wish you were gonna be here to see the railroad close down. Even the governor's gonna be here to hand me the deed. That sorry boy of ours is likely to sell it all, though. All he wants is dollars. He never did get his toes into the dirt like we did. Well, I gotta get going. After I get old Buster I'll have a few more years to keep the land away from that boy. I love 'im but sometimes I think he ain't got good sense.

She stood, walked through the house in her long flannel gown to the kitchen. Scrambled eggs and bacon, with last night's leftover biscuits and Georgia cane syrup, would keep her going all morning. Finished with breakfast, she took the time to wash up the dishes and frying pan, which she left to drain beside the sink.

Before returning to her bedroom to dress, she opened the kitchen door to check on the morning. Only a faint brightening to the east. Stars glittered. The crescent moon seemed tangled in the limbs of the persimmon tree.

Long time afore fly down.

Condensation under the tin roof dripped coolness on her arm. She listened, but heard only the silence of night.

For years, the flocks had roosted on the ridge just above Big Creek, in the high pines near the railroad. Last spring she had gone out to listen and anguish over not being out hunting. Buster ruled that roost last year. He was sure to still be king of the flock.

In another hour he'll be strutting on the old flat where they used to load up the cotton. Only open flat place around 'cept some of the farm roads. And the railroad bed.

She returned to her bedroom and dressed in camouflage. A dresser drawer yielded a pair of camouflage gloves and a netlike hood with eyeholes. She stuffed both into a pocket. She lifted Billy's hat from a hook above the dresser and tugged it over her white hair.

From the corner of the closet she lifted her shotgun. She broke it and looked down the barrel that gleamed from the last cleaning. She reached to the overhead shelf and took down the old box of shells, looked at the seven laid haphazardly inside. She removed only one, checked that it was a 2½-inch No.2 shot and slipped it into the chamber of the old Stevens .12 gauge single shot. *One turkey, one shot.*

She picked up the box call that she had chalked last night. The rag between the box and the striker kept it silent as she slipped it into a pocket.

With the shotgun dangling from one hand, she left for Buster's ridge as dawn backlit the trees. She strode with the steady confident stride that had carried her across the swamps with her father a lifetime ago.

A whip-poor-will shattered the silence as it flushed from the thickets she stepped by. She paused and listened for any sound that might awaken Buster, as she had done on the porch so many mornings since her son demanded she no longer hunt, no longer spend the silence of predawn in the woods, no longer see the birth of day and hear the earliest woodsongs out of sight and hearing of other humans. The woods weren't a lonely place, nowhere near as lonely as sitting in a crowd. Or standing on the porch at dawn.

A pair of geese rolled overhead against the dawning sky. A jay called and a crow answered. Buster gobbled, and the morning trembled.

"Humrpt" she grunted. "Still on that ridge." *Not as much time as I thought I had. He may be on the ground afore I get there. Late or not, any time is a good time to be out talking to turkeys.*

She felt alive with adrenalin and with the passion of again being alone in the woods. As a shadow blends against tree trunks, she became the shadows of leaves, trees, straw and vines. Compared with her iron skillets, the shotgun felt almost weightless. Her moccasined toes remembered to seek sticks before her weight fell onto each foot so no cracking would alert the woods. As she eased through the shadows, the restrictions imposed by her son and four walls slid away.

Gawd, it's been a long time. She emptied her mind of everything except the land around her and what would take her to the wild turkey—the scratched leaves, the white-edged droppings beneath a pine that served as a roost. A gobbler's roost. She smiled, remembering how her father had shocked her mother when he explained to his seven-year-old daughter the difference in tom and hen droppings by comparing their shapes to those of male and female sexual organs.

As Buster consumed her thoughts, the spring awakened around her—dogwoods lifted white petals like prayers to the morning, sunlight filtered through the new leaves to create a dream world of green, and wild azaleas flooded pinks and yellows across the hardwood bottom.

When he gobbled, she froze while her mind analyzed direction and volume. At the junction of the old cotton-wagon road and the railroad. At the old cotton loading dock. Only about two hundred yards away.

She hurried northward and, staying away from the railroad, kept behind thickets as she worked her way toward the crossing. When still a hundred yards away, she stopped against a pine and listened. Five minutes became ten and then twenty before Buster bellowed at the morning. Another gobbler echoed his call, and hens cackled back.

Looking for somewhere to hide within shotgun range of the railroad bed, she selected an oak twice as wide as her shoulders as a ready-made backrest. *Only twenty yards direct to the rails.* In seconds, she kicked out a swale at its base, perched her bottom onto the soft mulch remaining, and tested the sitting comfort and the view. It would do. Rising, she kicked leaves away from where her feet would be. A pocketknife snipped off a tiny dogwood that would tremble with any movement she made.

Can't have the bushes talking to Buster. Sitting, she pulled the shotgun tight against her shoulder and swung it from side to side, ensuring that the scattered small pines and vines in front of her were far enough away not to impede movement. She quickly slashed down the one pine that flicked against the barrel and stuck the pointed end into the ground a foot farther away to maintain some cover. She settled down, her knees pulled up to provide a rest for her shotgun and to shield her hands in her lap as she worked her box call. She tugged the face mask on, adjusted the eye holes, snugged Billy's cap down and slid her hands into the net gloves.

One series of *yelps*, so soft that only a turkey could hear it more than a few yards away, and Buster challenged the morning.

She waited. And waited. Would he move to meet the hen or demand that she come to him? Had he become so call-wise that he wouldn't respond? Was her skill with the cedar call still good enough to fool the youngsters if not Buster?

He gobbled again. She gave another two soft yelps.

Silence.

Far in the distance the train whistled, and Buster answered. Must be at Lawrence's Crossing, a good half-hour away.

Minutes seemed to be hours.

There he is!

A blob of black appeared beyond the understory, far beyond the range of her single shot. The shape widened, enlarged and became a semicircle of flared tail and dragging wings. Buster rotated one way and then back the other as he beckoned hens to his sunlit dance. Even at that distance the brilliant red of his head sent excitement surging through her. Buster *was* big.

Her heart rose into her throat, her pulse beat harder and harder until she tried to swallow. Her throat, filled with her heartbeat, didn't want to work. She gulped air, once, deeply, then again and again. The shotgun in her hands was shaking and heavy, her palms so wet they were slick. She wanted to rub her palms against her clothing, but knew she dared not move. The pulse in her throat rose into her head, pounded in her temples. Buster, as if he was aware of her reaction, dropped his tail, collapsed his strut, walked without concern along the tracks a few yards toward her and then blew up into another strut.

The old woman willed her body under control. The trembling stopped. Her throat accepted a swallow. The shotgun became light.

Three other toms appeared, fanning their tails each time he fanned. When he gobbled, they answered—knights to a king, yes-men to a corporate commander, lieutenants to a general, they each acknowledged Buster's command and dominance.

They moved toward her. Each time they swelled into a strut they carefully lifted one foot in her direction and then rotated in the slow courtship dance, with only each other and the old woman for an audience. The hens didn't show themselves if they were still behind the gobblers. Each time the toms dropped from strut, they walked two or three steps in her direction. Then they disappeared behind some thickets, still some seventy yards away.

She placed the box call on the ground. Too much calling had cost her several turkeys when she was young and impatient. Let him wonder and come looking.

Day moved forward faster than the birds, but the same patience that had kept her obedient to her father's demands in childhood now kept her body obedient to her mind as she willed herself to stay immobile. The toms would be close enough for her shot when they came back into sight. No-see-ums settled around her eyes. Mosquitoes found her, buzzed her face and feasted on her hands through the net. She felt something move down her collar—the feet of a tick crawling. Only her eyes moved, to blink away the insects. Sweat from her tension funneled down her face. Her hands, feeling the anticipation of her emotions, began to tremble and then steadied again as she pushed the tension down, turned her body away from it as she had turned away from the loneliness encroaching on her after Billy's death.

She took a deep breath, let it seep into her belly and lift her shoulders; she held it, savored it and slowly released it into the cloud of insects. She merged into the tree and into the ground. Her backside felt a vine she had not kicked away somewhere beneath the mulch, almost a knife slicing into her flesh. Every wave and edge in the bark behind her bit into her back. Her fingers locked around the shotgun, her thumb locked down on the hammer, and she eased it back while pressing lightly on the trigger to cock it silently. With her left hand propped against her left knee to hold the barrel steady, she pulled the stock tight against her right shoulder and rested her cheek on the stained wood, ready for Buster to strut into range.

A jay squawked at the toms, and silence approached as songbirds quieted ahead of the turkeys. The jay screamed again to herald the toms while warning the rest of the world to silence. A two-year old tom strolled in front, stopped near the pine she'd figured to be thirty yards away. He swelled into a strut, threw out his fan, pulled his head close to his chest, closed his eyes as if in ecstasy and slowly turned to show himself to whatever hens might be nearby. The morning sun caught bronzes, greens and reds like a kaleidoscope, ever changing.

Behind him came another tom, and then another, all larger than those she remembered from years ago, their heads red, white, blue and massive, their beards almost touching the ground. Their spurs shone black when they lifted their feet in the ritual dance.

One by one they passed the pine tree like a parade of prehistoric raptors, but Buster was not there. Mosquitoes dug into her hands through the netting and hovered around her eyes. No-see-ums delighted in an air battle with the mosquitoes. Her back throbbed; her legs ached; her hands went numb. She did not move.

Aware that a turkey could see her eyes blink at fifty yards, she squinted to keep from blinking.

Buster appeared, his head curled against his flared feathers, his tail spread like a fan across the horizon and his double beard dragging the crossties and gravel. His wings scratched loudly against wood and rocks. His waddle redder than blood throbbed with sexual excitement and anticipation. His drumming rolled to her, as loud as a dozen cats purring against her chest.

Oblivious to everything but himself, Buster strutted into full view.

She trembled as a warmth spread over her, the power of life and death, the need for taking this trophy of all trophies, the reality that here before her stood her only hope of escaping the nursing home.

Her heart hammered in her throat so loudly she feared he could hear as she breathed in all the way to her belly, slowly let the air out, swallowed once to moisten her throat. She had to pull Buster from his strut to have a target—no way she would take a chance on shooting him in full strut and only injuring him.

She whispered one *yelp* deep in her throat.

Buster's head shot up from his strut, his waddle almost exploding with red, his eyes expectant, searching, hopeful, anticipating.

She held the bead on the blood-red waddle, eased her thumb off the hammer and squeezed the trigger. She gave no thought to the frailty of her body or the power of the shotgun's kick.

Her follow-through as natural as a ball player letting his hand keep flowing to ensure accuracy, she kept the gun steady-on after the explosion. When she saw feathers flying, she pulled the shotgun down and rose to her feet in one continuous motion. Her body, flooded with adrenaline, forgot age and creaking joints. She leaped forward to claim her trophy.

On her fourth step, with the whistle of the governor's train blaring, she stepped into a stump hole. She fell forward, heard the crack as her leg broke and saw the train bearing down on the body of Buster lying in splendor between the rails.

Second Place: Tenth Annual Chattahoochee Valley Writers, 2016

THEN ALONG CAME SLIM

Kenny Stockton shivered. Sometimes he wondered why he loved being a ranger so much when it meant being this cold. Giving up a night's sleep never bothered him, especially on those nights when one of the idiots would think it was safe to kill a deer at 1:00 a.m. on one of the roads he patrolled.

Tonight he was backed up in a corner of an overseeded hay field where the fertilized silage lured deer from neighbors' yards to feed on the succulent new growth. The Texas wire gate lay pulled back where the poachers left it two nights ago. He thought surely they would return tonight.

But so far it had been quiet. No emergency calls from the TIP line and no calls on his personal or state cell phone. Just the call to hike his leg on a tire and hope he could bear the cold when he unzipped.

He reached back, flipped the switch to ensure the overhead light did not come on, opened the door and stepped out of the truck into the moonlit darkness. A deer blew at him, and four deer waved their white tails goodbye as they fled into the deeper darkness.

Well, those four won't be here for the poachers tonight.

He tended to business and stretched to relieve some of the kinks in his back. His legs announced they were tired of his sitting, and he locked his knees, touched his toes ten times and jogged in place. In spite of the activity, he shivered.

He stepped to the front of the truck and leaned back against the hood's warmth. As the heat penetrated his coat, he studied the stars, sought the Pleiades that his mother had so often pointed out to him with a flashlight as they lay on a blanket in the hayfield. Remembering, he smiled and looked eastward, to see Orion slipping upward. The belt showed, but the sword still lay hidden beyond the horizon.

Far to the west, a rifle sounded once, the sound softer than a tennis ball bounce. Kenny straightened, stepped back into the truck and keyed his radio. "Sixteen, this is Nine. You hear that?"

"Yeah. I'm on it. Right in my back yard. I'll call if I need backup."

"Roger. And out."

Kenny smiled. Dusty would have those culprits down to the jail in less time than it would take a crow to fly the distance. *Besides, a crow would stop at that pecan grove for a snack before it flew the distance.*

Kenny reached for his Thermos, unscrewed the top, but hesitated. *Better not. I don't want to have to hike my leg again.*

He retightened the cap and placed the Thermos back on the passenger seat. Far in the distance, he saw headlights top the hill at the Dennis place. The vehicle slowed as it came down the hill.

Here we go. One for Dusty tonight, and now one for me. He rolled down the windows. Excitement similar to buck fever roared through him as the vehicle approached the gate and turned into the field.

"Com'on guys. Just a bit more."

A spotlight came out of the passenger window and swept the field.

Kenny cranked up, flipped his blue lights on and pulled out of his hidey-hole between the truck and the gate.

"Damn it!"

The poacher's curse reached Kenny, and he chuckled. The culprit made no attempt to flee, but turned off the engine and stepped out as Kenny pulled up behind him.

No weapon in his hand.

Kenny slid out of his truck, his flashlight in one hand and his other hand resting on the butt of his pistol. The passenger might not be so agreeable.

"We're just looking at the deer," the driver said. He turned toward the truck and continued, "Ain't that so, Bill?"

Bill climbed out of the passenger seat. "That's so."

He held no weapon. Kenny's stomach relaxed.

"Uh-huh. Well, let's see. You fellows step to the front of your truck there." They did.

"I need your ID." The men pulled out their wallets and extended them toward Kenny.

"Just take out your driver's licenses. I don't need the wallets."

They each pulled out the laminated cards and handed them to Kenny.

"You got any weapons on you? Pistol? Knife?"

"No sir," the driver responded.

"I got a knife," Bill said and pointed to his waist.

Kenny checked them over and found only the buck knife on Bill's belt. He slid the knife out of its sheath and walked to the back of the truck to place it in truck bed.

He dropped the tailgate. Moonlight glistened on fresh blood in the grooves of the liner.

"Where's the deer?" he asked as he turned the flashlight onto the faces of the two men.

"Whatcha mean? We don't have a deer."

"Well, not now, but the one you killed earlier tonight?"

"We ain't killed no deer."

"I reckon all this blood in the tailgate means you killed somebody? You better hope it's deer blood, not people blood. Night hunting is a lot less serious than murder."

"We ain't killed nobody!" the driver yelled.

"Okay. Then where's the deer?"

Neither answered. "Okay. I'll find it."

Kenny searched the truck and found a .44 Ruger rifle, loaded, with a cartridge in the chamber. The safety on. A .12 gauge Remington was also propped against the seat between driver and passenger. A half-filled box of shotgun shells lay on the seat. He moved all to his truck.

"Okay, guys, we're going to the jail. You know where it is, over on Shirley Drive? Off Washington Street?"

"Yessir," the driver said.

"You lead, I'll follow. You're under arrest for night hunting."

On the way to the jail, Kenny raised Dusty on the radio. He was just leaving the jail. Kenny gave him addresses for the two men and asked Dusty to check their homes for a deer.

By the time Kenny reached the jail, Dusty radioed he had found the deer.

"Case made and closed," Kenny responded. "You want-a take it to the Hunters for the Hungry?" Dusty did.

Faced with the evidence, the two men admitted to night hunting and lost their truck, spotlight and weapons. "You can buy them back from the judge when you go to trial," Kenny explained to them. "And call a cab to get home. Usual fine in this county is a thousand for night hunting and another thousand for hunting on private lands without permission. You boys will have a lot to pony up. It'll probably cost another two or three for the truck and weapons. Our judge doesn't like night hunters."

Satisfied that he had done a good night's work, Kenny started for home. Not bad. He'd be in bed by 4:00 a.m.

Frost had settled on his truck windshield and he had to take time to clean it off. Even the heater had to warm up again. Twelve miles later, he had turned into his driveway when his radio squawked. Dispatch was looking for Dusty.

Dusty didn't answer—he had gone home.

"Kenny, you copy?"

The ranger clicked on his mike. "Ten four. What's up?"

"Gunfire report on Highway 212. What's your 20?"

"Oh, gads. In my driveway. North or south of the fire station?"

"South. Near the McIntyes."

No wonder I didn't hear it. My window's closed. "I got it. No need to telephone Dusty. He's likely in bed."

They're not more than three miles away. Leave off the noise. I don't want to let 'em know I'm coming.

At four a.m., only poachers and deer would be on the road. He gunned the state vehicle to ninety on the mile-long straight-away, and as he neared the curve at the power station, he dropped to a safer forty.

And skidded to a stop.

A beer van, turned sideways on the left shoulder, blocked half of that lane, its headlights showing two men dragging a deer from the edge of the pines onto the twenty-foot stretch of cleared land under the power lines.

Kenny flipped on his flashing lights and parked parallel on the opposite shoulder. The men continued toward the van, the size of the twelve-point trophy deer keeping their progress slow.

The thin man on Kenny's left carried a lever-action 30-30 in his right hand while holding onto the buck's antler with his left. The other man, very overweight, walked sideways, both hands grasping the other antler. He grunted with each step.

"Slim and the Fat Man. Again," Kenny muttered. He stepped out of the truck and hitched up his belt, heavy with his pistol, radio and billy club. He didn't want to have to arrest these two men again. It seemed like they would know better than to use the beer van. He'd have to confiscate it and Fat Man would lose his job. Again.

"Hold it there, men. It's Ranger Stockton. You're both under arrest for spotlighting."

The men stopped. Slim released the deer and its weight pulled Fat Man to his knees.

Kenny stepped into the glare of the van's headlights.

"You ain't taking me to any jail, Kenny. Not no more." Slim swung the 30-30 to his shoulder.

"Don't do this, Slim." The muzzle of the 30-30 looked bigger than the end of a .12 gauge. Kenny dropped flat as he pulled out his pistol and swung it forward.

The rifle shot went over him.

He shot Slim in the knee.

Slim screamed, fell, gripped his knee and rocked with pain.

Fat Man yelled and ran into the woods.

Kenny scrambled to his feet, holstered his pistol, and ran to Slim.

"Get away from me, you effing bastard. You gonna pay for this."

Stockton halted. He saw the pain in Slim's face, but knew the problems he faced for shooting a suspect. He pulled out his hand-kerchief, retrieved the rifle and moved it fifteen feet away.

Slim and the Fat Man would lie, as always, but at least the spent shell in the chamber would prove he shot Slim in self defense.

He radioed for backup and an ambulance. Going home and sleep would not be options tonight. The State Bureau of Investigation would take his weapon and demand the details of the night. Slim would get Lawyer Jackson and sue.

Oh gawd don't let me lose this job.

THE WORLD RECORD BASS

Kyle always fished alone, even in the bass battle in Lake Sinclair in middle Georgia. He signed in and the sponsors checked his license and equipment to ensure he met the requirements. He backed his trailer down the ramp, lowered his customized Ranger bass boat into the water, secured it to the dock, and parked his truck and trailer in the shade of an oak. By noon it would be in the sun.

He stepped into his boat, untied the mooring line and cranked his Honda BF 250. He eased through the no-wake zone and then roared off into the rising mist of the early July dawn.

He knew where the big bass lurked, in a cove where he had seen no fishermen in the two years he had worked his way around the lake. Last summer, however, he had caught the largest bass of his life there—weighing in at 22 pounds even. He had released it.

He knew he would catch *Monster* again today. It should have gained enough to beat Perry's twenty-two pound four-ounce world record from June 1932. He needed only time in the cove. And the right bait.

He was loaded with bait and tackle. Two MicroWave System rods with WaveSpin reels. *Nothing as good as what Doug Hannon designed.* A cane pole with nylon line that he planned to use to catch his live bait. A can of night crawlers to lure in the bait.

He met two boatloads of local early risers out for water skiing but otherwise the lake surface only rippled with the breeze from the distant Gulf. A few thin clouds drifted ahead of the wind. Not enough to bring rain but also not enough to shade him. To avoid the increasing heat of day, when he reached his cove after a forty-five minute ride, he anchored at the edge of the shadow line. He would move with the shadows of the pines and oaks as they shrank toward the bank. He hoped to have his fish before the heat became too oppressive.

He pulled a night crawler from the can of mulch and hooked it on-to the cane pole line. No weight on the line, just his bobber set for the hook to be no more than two feet under. He cast toward the bank, watched the line drop about ten feet out. He settled down to wait.

He did not check his watch. Time would be irrelevant today.

The bobber disappeared. "That was fast," he said.

He tugged to set the hook and pulled the bream to the boat. "You are perfect," he said as he twisted the hook out of its mouth. He converted it into bait on one of the rod-and-reel setups. He studied the area and remembered last summer.

He cast to the deep water several yards beyond the end of the fallen tree, to where he had hooked the monster last summer. He stuck the handle of the rod into a clip on the boat.

The bait fish pulled the bobber under and around. He watched and nodded. "That'll do for one kind of live action. I'll just add more live action with my lure. One or the other's gonna bring the monster home."

Kyle opened his tackle box and took out his treasure. He had found three Creek Chub Bait Company lures online and paid almost one thousand dollars for the three. He lifted out the fintail shiner.

He caressed the back of the lure as if it were a favorite puppy. *You cost me a fortune, but if you are as inviting as Perry's was, you'll bring that monster back to me. Let's get you in the water and you do your stuff. I need to win this tourney.*

He laid the rod across his lap and snipped the end of the line. *No swivel means no chance of one getting pulled open and letting the hook free. I'll just tie my fintail on. Triple knot.*

He cast away from the bank and the fallen tree to get the feel of the weight of the lure. *I could put it on a quarter out there. No wonder everybody wants one. Not just because it caught the world's record but it is a dream lure.*

But I can't just cast into the open lake. Got to concentrate on the area of the old tree. Just don't catch a limb bream.

His bait fish tugged at that bobber. His fintail glided through the water like a child's dream of Christmas.

The sun climbed higher. So did the temperature. He pulled in three bass and released them all. He weighed the largest one on his hand-held scale. Nine pounds. *I ain't out here to catch a passel of little ones. I want just one. Just the one from last summer. I know it's still here or it'd have been in the news all over the country.*

His first cast after releasing the nine pounder, the lure seemed to have caught on a limb of the rotting tree. He worked the line, the rod and reel. It moved. But barely.

I got to get this limb up to the boat. I can't lose that lure. Not with what it cost me.

Slowly it moved. The surface rippled. He lifted the end of the rod to tighten the line and lowered it as he wound it in a few inches. After five minutes of struggle, he gasped.

The monster rose from the water, sat on his tail and danced.

Kyle pulled the line taunt and lowered the end of the rod to pull Monster down into the water.

Oh dear gussie. Don't let him shake the hook out.

He kept up the pattern of lifting the rod and reeling as he lowered it. The monster appeared just off the port side of the boat. Kyle pushed the butt of the rod into his belly, gripped the handle of the reel and reached for the net.

He swept the net behind the fish and up. As the net enclosed the monster, he dropped the rod, seized the net with both hands and lifted.

He brought the net into the boat and dropped the fish onto the deck.

He would go in the record books, be remembered for a hundred years. He had caught a fish larger than any other bass in the world.

He dropped to his knees on the deck and pulled the net off the thrashing fish.

"Easy now, fella. I'll just get that hook out of your mouth and put you back in water, but not in the lake this time. This time, you'll go in the livewell and back to the judge with me. You'll be the most famous fish in America today."

He gripped the fish under its jaw and reached inside the mouth to remove the hook.

"Oh my gawd, what is that?"

He pulled his right hand out of the fish's mouth and stared at his forefinger. Two dots showed blood.

"What in hell?"

He lifted the fish enough to look in its mouth. A snake stared back at him. He dropped the fish.

"Damn Sam. I never heard of such. Must be a moccasin. What've I got to make a tourniquet? Got a fillet knife. That'll let the poison drain."

He gritted his teeth as he sliced a line between the two fang marks. He bled freely. He cut the line from the fish's mouth, twisted it around his wrist several times and cut it free from the reel.

As he let the rod drop, the snake slithered from the fish's mouth. He snatched his emergency paddle from its clips on the side and whacked the snake across the back. It wriggled. He shoved the paddle blade beneath the snake and tossed it overboard.

He dumped the fish into the thirty-one gallon livewell and reeled in the bait bream. "Gotta get to the dock and get some antivenom. I'll call ahead."

He reached in his cargo pants pocket for his phone. It wasn't there. He closed his eyes and remembered—he had talked to his son just before he got out of the truck. It was on the front seat of his pickup.

"Gotta go."

The motor roared to life and he set out for the dock. He handled the boat with his left hand. The right hand had swollen and turned blue. "It's lose my hand or lose my life. Damn snake."

Twenty minutes out in the open water, he spotted another fisherman and hailed him. Kyle cut his motor and the two boats drifted together.

"Man, what happened to you?" the man asked.

"Got moccasin bit. You got anything I can use for a tourniquet? All I've got is this fishing line. And I got to take it off or it's gonna cut off my hand."

"Sure don't, but I can call ahead for you. They can have you some help when you get to the dock. You get antivenom you'll be okay. But you better get that line from around your wrist or you won't have a hand left."

"Thanks. I came out without my phone. Please do. I don't think I can get this line off now. It's swollen into my wrist. I'd rather be dead than not able to fish."

"Let me help you."

They threw lines to each other and tied the boats together. Kyle left his in idle. The other man stepped across. "I'm Turner Jenkins," he said.

"I'm Kyle Warren."

"How did you get bit?"

"I caught the biggest damn fish ever and it had caught a moccasin but only half-swallowed it. I stuck my hand in to get out the hook and got bit."

Turner shook his head. "Weird. I have heard of such, though." He took Kyle's hand and began to study the string. "I found an end here. I'll pull it around. Hang on. It may hurt."

"You're right. It does. "

"What did you catch?"

"It's in the livewell. Biggest fish ever. It'll be a world record."

"Yeah? May I look?"

"Sure." Kyle opened the top of the livewell.

"My good God man. I never seen such a fish."

Turner bent down for a closer look. He shook his head. "I can't believe it. You're gonna win this tourney and get famous forever."

He stood up, looked around the boat, and held his hand out to Kyle.

"Congratulations," he said.

Kyle took his hand.

Turner jerked. Kyle stumbled. Turner shoved him overboard.

"Sorry, Kyle."

He pushed Kyle's throttle from idle to forward and left Kyle bobbing in the water. With the boats tied together, his banged and slammed Kyle's as he raced away.

Two hundred yards off, he stopped. He looked at Kyle's tackle and threw both rods onto the deck of his boat. He pulled the monster from the livewell, slipped his fingers into the gills, and stepped into his own boat. He put the fish into his livewell. He untied Kyle's boat from his and pushed the throttle on Kyle's boat as far forward as it would go. The boat roared off.

Turner headed for the dock to claim Kyle's victory and world record. He never looked back. As soon as he tied up his boat, he leaped onto the dock and shouted. "I got a new world's record!"

The three judges rushed over him.

"It's in the livewell. Where abouts are the scales? I don't want it to lose an ounce while I wait for the scales."

"We got paperwork to do first," Len, the chief judge said. "You have your entry papers?"

Turner reached into the side pocket of his cargo pants and pulled out a leather folder. He flipped it open and slid out the paper.

Len glanced it over and handed it back. "Looks good. Now we need to see your tackle."

Turner stepped back into the boat and lifted up Kyle's rod and reel, with the lure attached. "This is what I caught it on."

Len took the tackle and began to make notes on the make of each part—rod, reel, lure. He commented, "I see you are a fan of Doug Hannon."

"Who?"

"Doug Hannon. Oh, man. What didcha pay for this lure?"

"Nothing much. I don't remember exactly. Got it over to the fishing store up the road."

Len frowned. *No way Turner got this lure there. Maybe online, like Kyle did. But at the fishing store for not much? This is a five hundred dollar lure, not made for years.*

"You positive this is one you bought locally?"

Turner shrugged. "Yeah. Positive."

Len turned away and spoke to the other two judges, "Something's wrong. This is a Creek Chub fintail. Very special. Very expensive. Only person who left here with one of these was Kyle Warren. And look," he pointed to the base of the handle, to the *KW* scratched in the metal with a knife point. "This has to be Kyle's tackle. Let's get the fish, weigh it, and keep it in a livewell until Kyle comes in."

They agreed. Len laid the fish on the scales and said, "By God, it is a record! Look guys! It's twenty-three pounds and four ounces. Hey, what's that boatman think he's doing?" He turned from the scales to see a Chris-Craft coming in hard. "He's going too fast. This is a no wake area."

The Chris-Craft continued toward the dock and as it neared, it stopped suddenly and then eased to the dock. A man lay on the back seat.

Len rushed over. The driver yelled, "I've called the police and an ambulance. Kyle here nearly drowned and has been snake bit."

Footsteps pounded on the dock. Len looked back to see Turner fleeing toward the parking lot.

Kyle sat up and screamed, "What is that?"

They all turned. A bald eagle swooped down to the scales and sank its talons into the monster. He flapped his wings and tried to lift the fish.

"Oh God no," Kyle screamed. He tried to scramble from the boat and fell. Mike and Len yelled, waved their hands and rushed to the scales where the eagle struggled. The eagle lifted off, rose two feet into the air and lost its grip on the fish.

Monster fell into the water and sank.

Thanks to Bill Vanderford for help with information on fishing lore, tackle, boats and Doug Hannon. Bill is a retired professional fishing guide in Georgia and a member of the Fishing Guides Hall of Fame.

TILTING STONE MOUNTAIN

She looked at the message again. All she had asked for was an address, but instead of just the address the reply rambled on about what the e-mail might contain—grits, sand, dead insects, tools from the garage.

Well, at least it didn't give my computer a bug. This guy must be nuts. I'll give it back to him.

She replied, "Thanks. Please next time we write, send me a shovel. I need a new one. I broke the metal handle on the last one when I used it to tilt Stone Mountain."

She didn't even know the jokester, but couldn't help herself. If he could be silly, so could she.

A few days later, she had to e-mail him again. She didn't write a new message, but went to their previous notes and replied. At the end of the message, she added, "I still need a new shovel."

He replied, and at the end of the business portion of his e-mail, he added, "See attachment for your shovel."

Business tended to, she downloaded the attachment and opened it. Picture of a metal-handled shovel. She printed the picture and when the printer ejected the paper, she lifted it and stood up. The paper trembled in her hand and grew heavy.

She stared. Her hand gripped a metal shovel and a blank piece of paper.

"Well, I'll be damned if that isn't something. I'm going to Stone Mountain. Maybe it really will tilt the big rock."

The shovel was heavier than she remembered hers. She hadn't used it in years, not since she had left it, forgotten, on her back patio and a burglar had used it to bust open a downstairs window. He had made it inside when the alarm sounded and he fled, taking nothing but his own fear with him. She had parked that shovel in the back of the garage where it had gathered dust for seven years.

She folded the paper to throw away, but when she did, the shovel vanished. She unfolded the paper and here came the shovel. *I can get in the gate with the shovel and no one will ever know.*

She sat back down and searched *Stone Mountain*. She ran down the listings until she found one with a good picture of the carvings. She printed the picture to take with her.

At the entrance to the park, she was waved in—her window decal announced to the world that she belonged in the park.

She exited her SUV and took both sheets of paper with her toward the side of the mountain. She noticed more staff members around than she used to see, back before it became a privately operated public park. When she unfolded her papers and the shovel appeared, so did a staff member.

He approached and asked, "What's the shovel for, Ma'am? You can't dig up flowers in the park. Or anything else for that matter."

"Oh, I know. It's just to use to tilt the big rock."

"To what?"

"You know. Tilt the rock. So our soldiers don't just seem to be riding along on level ground. They need to be seen riding uphill. After all, their battles mostly had them going uphill, especially near the end of The War."

The staffer laughed. "Well, if you think you can tilt the mountain, you go right ahead. May I watch?"

She shrugged. "Sure."

She propped the shovel against a tree and unfolded the picture of the carving. She studied the picture and the mountain, picked up the shovel and moved a few yards to the left.

Where stone met dirt, she stopped and surveyed the area. "Right here," she muttered. She turned back to the staffer. "You might want to back up a bit. I don't know how much ground will be disturbed when the rock tilts."

"Oh, I think I'll be fine," he said. She noticed the laughter he tried to swallow.

"Well, don't say I didn't warn you."

She angled the point toward the base of the mountain and stuck the shovel into the ground. She lined the images of the soldiers exactly with the images on the mountain and turned it slightly, so the images seemed to be riding uphill. She held the paper in one hand and reached for the shovel with the other.

"Slow as Leap year," she said. She placed one foot on the shovel and applied pressure until the shovel blade was buried. She double-checked the angle of the picture and eased back on the shovel handle.

The earth trembled. The staffer fled. The rock shuddered. She smiled as the mountain titled to match the image. Lee, Jackson and Davis now charged uphill.

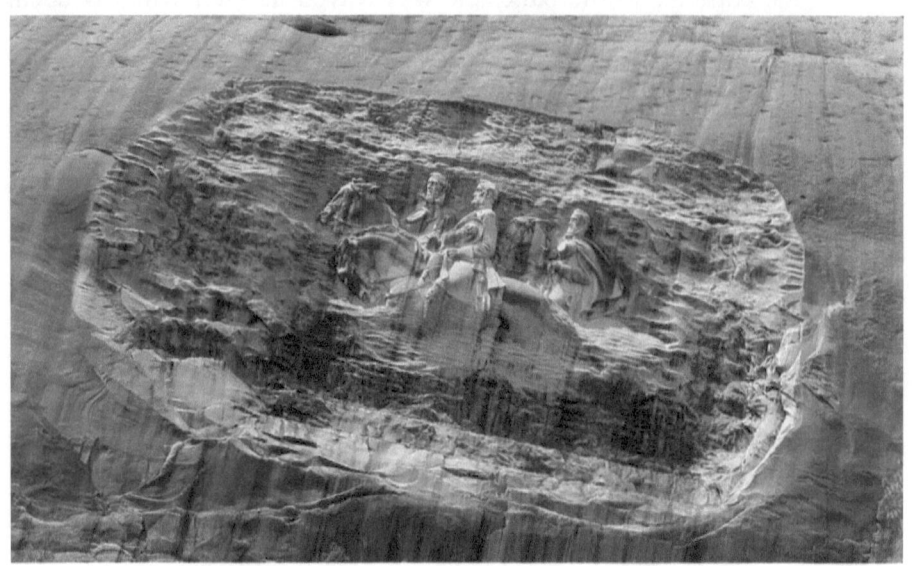

She folded the papers. The shovel disappeared and its image reappeared on the paper. She piled back into her SUV to drive home, and when she turned on the radio to WSB an announcer interrupted the talk show to yell about the massive earthquake centered at Stone Mountain.

With thanks to Ben R. Baker(editor and general manager of The Wiregrass Farmer) *who stated his e-mail might carry various items with it.*

"MISTAKEN" ID

Maryanne heard the machines in the distance and ignored them while she renewed her acquaintance with her own acres. Fall wildflowers should be blooming. Crab apples would be dropping. Muscadines would perfume the land. She wanted to visit her autumn woods before the deer and birds consumed all the fruit. She had reached home last night after ten weeks in the west on her childhood dream trip—hiking in Yellowstone with her camera and catching images of elk in rut, of eagles gripping fish in their talons, of pairs of frisky otters playing in Yellowstone River. Glacier Park still had flowers blooming through ice and glaciers dripping into pools.

The machines pulled her thoughts from the past weeks to the present. Whatever was growling and beeping as it backed up was too close. Sounded like bulldozers. She stopped on the ridge and listened, but the sounds died. *Whatever that was, whoever it is, they must-a stopped for lunch.*

Another sound reached her, leaves disturbed. She closed her eyes and listened. Not a squirrel's hopping. Too loud for a fox, but foxes wouldn't be out and about at noon. She eased her head to look to her right and squinted into the sun. *Ah, a deer. Two. Doe and spring fawn out of its spots.*

Mama spotted her and bounded away with the fawn close behind.

I hope these never get as tame as the ones in the parks out west. I could pet the mule deer in California if I'd wanted to.

She continued her walk, crossed the ridge and strode down to Rocky Branch. As she entered the hardwoods that flanked the stream and grew almost to the top of the ridge, she turned to her left and headed down to the hollow, to the red mulberry trees where the deer fed on the leaves.

But before she reached the mulberry trees, the bulldozer cranked up again. Its roar reached her from over the next ridge. *Either they're working on the highway or somebody's on my land.* Only her acreage lay in that direction, to the highway and across it to another thousand acres.

She abandoned her trip to the mulberry trees and turned toward the sound. Her ambling turned to the same strong stride that had carried her across miles every day when she was home, as well as on the recent trip.

She hurried up the next ridge, and when she topped it, she stopped dead and stared. Below her, acres had been bulldozed. Several houses neared completion. The creek was already backing up in a pond that appeared to flood at least ten acres.

By God, somebody has the wrong map. And somebody is gonna pay dearly for what they've done. This is supposed to be wildlife land, not some housing project.

She reached her right hand to the holster she never left home without, lifted the .38 Smith and Wesson revolver, broke it to check her loads, snapped it to, flipped the safety off and back on, and shoved it back into the holster.

She stomped downhill, across the torn land and directly into the path of the bulldozer. She raised both hands, palms toward the driver. He stopped.

She signaled for him to dismount. He did so and stormed to her.

"What's with you, lady?" he yelled as she strode toward him.

"What do you mean, *what's with me*? What's with you? What do you think you're doing here? This is my land."

"No way, lady. You go talk to the gentleman over yonder." He pointed to a man in jeans, white shirt and hard hat who stood talking to a carpenter on the porch of one of the buildings already dried in. To her it looked big enough to be a hotel.

Anger drove her to the man in the hard hat. "What's going on here? This is my land."

"No, Ma'am. We bought it fair and square. We bought two hundred acres here two months ago."

"Not from me, you didn't. I was in Kansas two months ago."

"Lady, I don't know who you are, but we have a signed deed. You want to talk to the lawyers about this, go ahead, but I've work to do. Please go away."

"I'll see you in court is what I'll do. But in jail first."

She headed for home, her mind twirling. No way they had a deed. She'd never sell an acre. *I'm going to leave it all as a wildlife sanctuary. Never to be sold. How can these people have a deed when I wasn't even here two months ago?*

She didn't bother to go inside when she reached home. She climbed into her blue Subaru Outback and headed to town and the courthouse. *Might need to see the attorney, but I'm gonna find out about their deed first.*

She found the deed. Signed and recorded and not her signature. But her name. She asked the clerk to copy it for her and with the copy in hand she went to see her cousin, daughter of her father's twin brother. Like her, the other Maryanne was still unmarried.

Maryanne Emily was home and welcomed her. "You look hot and tired. How about some iced tea?"

"Sounds great."

They settled down in rockers on the front porch. "You look like you've lost weight, Maryanne Emily."

"I have. I lost about twenty pounds while you were gone." She went on to tell about her appendix rupturing, the storm that flooded the road so the ambulance couldn't get to her for hours. "It was a rough time in the hospital. I don't even remember the first few days. The EMTs had to carry me out of the house. I mean literally. That's about all I remember—that cute young man picking me up and toting me down the steps. I do remember the surgeon telling one of the nurses he was glad to see me doing so well, he had expected to lose me." She laughed. "I bet he was afraid I'd die and not pay my bill."

"Well, I came home last night and discovered a problem. Not nearly as bad as your appendix, though. I found a construction crew merrily building houses and a lake on a section of my land off Mary Annette Drive."

Maryanne Emily stopped rocking. "You got to be kidding."

"Nope. They told me they had a deed. I went by the courthouse, got a copy. And it's got my name on it all right." She grinned. "I reckon they got to you while you were drunk out of your head with that surgery and thought you were me because our names are the same, and they got you to sign it. You remember anything about the papers you had to sign?"

Maryanne Emily shook her head. "I just remember a lot of papers. I don't know. I just can't remember much. I do remember a nurse brought me some papers and I think some lady in a suit came with some men with some papers. I just don't know."

Maryanne pulled out the deed. "It says they paid four million for the land. I wonder where the money is."

The cousin shook her head. "I've no idea. I wonder if they put it in your bank account? It wouldn't have been in mine because I always use

M. Emily to keep from confusing the tellers."

Maryanne stood up. "Great idea. I haven't even been to the post office yet for my mail. I should have a bank statement there, but I'll go to the bank first. I am so glad you didn't up and die on me while I was gone."

The cousins hugged and Maryanne left for the bank.

She entered and headed to the manager's office, but before she said anything, he rose and met her at the door, his hand extended. She took it as he said. "Well, I'm glad to see you. We got quite a surprise with that check you mailed us."

"Ah-ha. Mystery solved."

"Mystery?"

"Yeah, Ted. Some crooks tricked my cousin into signing a deed she thought was hospital admission papers. Maybe they thought she was I. Who knows. So they sent you a check for my account, did they?"

Ted's face paled. He nodded.

"Can you make me a copy of the deposit?"

With her hands full of papers, she hied down the street to Wilbur's office. Let her attorney handle affairs now.

After she gave him a brief summary, he replied, "Well, we have them over a barrel. What do you want to do?"

She smiled. "Well, the more they invest out there, the more they have to lose. I'll go back to them and tell them the truth. If they refuse to accept it, then I say let them work away until we file in court. I hate to forsake the acreage, but I'll gladly accept the improvements. I can afford to complete whatever is unfinished. It'll make great housing for our homeless veterans."

She drove back to the construction site. The same man spotted her as she stepped out of the car. "What do you want now?" He almost snarled at her.

"Well, here's the situation. I didn't sign this deed. A cousin did. As I said before, I wasn't even in the state at the time." She held the document toward him.

"Yeah? Who cares? She has a Power of Attorney and can sell when you're gone. We checked it at the courthouse."

Maryanne smiled. "Not quite. Only when I'm *incapacitated and unable to act for myself.*" She made quote marks with her fingers. "Being on vacation doesn't apply."

"Lady, just go away. I've got work to do."

"You better be talking to your attorney. The longer you stay here, the more your company is going to lose in the long run."

"You are trespassing. I've asked you to leave. If you don't, I'll have you arrested."

She smiled. "Fine. I'll see you in court."

Wilbur searched financial records to trace ownership of the corporation that "purchased" the land. Ownership was tiered through several wealthy real estate businesses.

Two months after Maryanne's return from her trip, the case was filed and announced to the press. The next day, national media invaded the town to report on the story of the national corporation that had coaxed a women on her maybe-deathbed to sign a paper she thought related to her medical care but was in fact a deed to sell her same-named cousin's land.

Three months later, the corporation's attorneys asked for a hearing. Wilbur did not object. They asked for the case to be dismissed. The judge laughed and shook his head. "Not a chance."

The trail began six weeks later. Maryanne sat beside Wilbur as *voir dire* took place for three days. Wilbur accepted everyone. The corporation tried to strike everybody.

Wilbur called only three witnesses, two Maryannes and the banker. As the court recessed for the weekend, the other attorneys asked Wilbur if he would settle for the four million paid for the land.

"I don't think so," he replied.

"Will you let the judge decide on the settlement rather than the jury?"

Wilbur pondered and said he would ask his client and get back to them. He told Maryanne the jury might give her more, "But Judge Perkins hates this kind of action. It's up to you."

She went for the judge.

Attorneys spent the weekend preparing paperwork for Judge Perkins. Maryanne walked over to the construction site. All work had stopped.

Monday afternoon, she, Wilbur and the three attorneys stood before the bench and awaited the judgment.

Judge Perkins looked from Wilbur to the corporate attorneys. "I see from your filings you both have agreed that my decision will not be subject to appeal."

"Yes, Your Honor." The three spoke in unison.

"Wilbur? What about you? Accept and not appeal?"

"Yes, Your Honor."

"Well," Perkins began what Wilbur expected to be one of his long dialogs about right and wrong. Instead, he was brief. "I find what you did," he looked at the corporate men, "to be appalling and disgusting. To trick a sick woman into signing a deed while thinking she was signing a medical release is beyond the pale. I hereby find for the plaintiffs. I don't like fraud or what even appears to be fraud. You jokers put four million into a bank account in the real owner's name without even telling her. Maybe you thought you had the right person. Maybe not. In any case, the four million stays. Actual damages to two hundred acres of pristine wildlife habitat and old growth timber is beyond my ability to appraise. But you corporate men put the actual value at four million, so we'll call that the actual damage to Miss Maryanne's land. Punitive damages we'll put at another ten million. You also finish plumbing, wiring, insulating and drying in all structures, drill a well and hook up water to all structures. Seed the bare land with rye and clover to ensure no erosion, put bales of hay along any drains, and then get off the land."

"You got all that?" he asked the court reporter.

"Yes, sir."

"Good, type it up and give both parties a copy."

He banged his gavel, rose and left the courtroom.

Wilbur turned to Maryanne. He was grinning from ear to ear. He had just earned thirty per cent of fourteen million and could go to Florida for spring training if he could just get tickets to the Red Sox in their new stadium. Might cost a bit, but now, who cared?

"Looks like we win," he said.

"Yeah. Now let's see about the homeless vets. Take a look at the houses underway and see what we will need for furnishings to make them suitable when the company's work is finished. From what I've seen, we can house four men in each one. We'll set up a foundation with all of this money. You don't mind contributing your thirty per cent to the veterans, do you? You can run the foundation and see to everything, and even get a token salary from the foundation."

HIGH HOPES

The half-hound, half-terrier lay in shade cast by a chinaberry tree whose purple blooms perfumed the spring air. The screen door of the clapboard house opened and a woman stepped out.

Her dress about matched the house. Paint peeled in curls from the siding, and her feedsack dress showed two triangular rips curling from the side of the skirt. She rattled the car keys in her left hand and carried a worn cloth purse over her right arm.

She went to the faded two-tone-green Pontiac, opened the front passenger door and hand-cranked the window down. She turned toward the chinaberry tree.

"Com'on, Dog."

Oh boy. She's asking me to get in. Oh, oh. All my life I wanted to get in the car and go with her, wherever she goes all day. Oh joy! Now I can! She loves me at last.

The pooch leaped up and carried a dust cloud as he rushed to the car and leaped in.

She slammed the door, circled the car and slid into the driver's seat. The dog pushed his head toward her. She shoved him back.

"Oh, no, you don't, Dog."

He turned to the window and poked his head out into the wind. And sniffed.

Maybe I can't sit in her lap, but it's my first time in the car. She didn't even mention fleas and ticks. Maybe I can go inside the house today too.

The dog pulled his head inside and scratched behind his left ear.

"Damn. I should'a sprayed you for those fleas. I'll have them in the car. Good thing I never let you in the house."

I want to lick her face but I don't dare. Besides I want to see everywhere we go and smell everything outside too.

I smell pizza. Maybe that's the place it comes from. She always throws me a slice. Even when it lands in the dirt, just like the bones she pitches to me, I don't care. The dirt doesn't hurt the flavor of the cheeses or the meat or the wonderful inside of the bones when I crack them. I wish we could stop and get some pizza.

I smell the pie she sometimes lets me lick out of the pan when they finish it. That must be where it comes from. I am so lucky to get this ride.

Why are we stopping? There's nothing here. Not a house. Not a store. Just wide open road with a lot of green fields stretching way off. The biggest yard ever. I wonder where the people are who must live here.

All I see are big animals with their heads down and with black spots all over them. I'm black too, but I don't have spots. My ears are slim and pointed and won't stand up, but their big ones stand off to the side of their heads.

Oh my, one of them has picked up her head and is sticking her tongue up one side and then the other of her nose. I can't begin to do that. And there's a little one sucking on her titties and butting its head up against her belly.

"Let's go, Dog," she says when she opens the door.

She gets out and I scramble out behind her. We're going for a walk. I bounce up and down to let her know how happy I am.

She closes the door and walks almost all the way around the car. I bounce along behind her.

"No. Get back." She swings a foot at the dog and he jumps back.

He sits and wags his tail.

I wag my tail so she'll know I didn't mean to annoy her. But why is she mad? All I've done is what she asked me to.

She jerks open the door, scrambles in and closes it. The dog runs to the door, stands up and paws it with both front feet. She tears off down the road. He barks.

Why is she leaving me? What did I do? I can't run any more. She's gone. I can't even see the car. How can I get home? We turned so many times.

An eighteen-wheeler blares and goes by with so much wind the dog rolls into the ditch. He scampers up and onto the road.

Here comes a car now. Maybe it's her. No, it's white and hers is dark.

He sits near the ditch and watches cars. She does not return.

She didn't want me. It was all a mean trick to throw me away. But somebody will want me. Here comes somebody. Maybe....Oh, it's going so fast! Slow down. Stop. Don't you want me to go home with you?

It slows, slews around me and speeds up. Another one comes on the other side of the in-between yard. I run toward it, but it veers away and leaves me smelling its exhaust.

The smell makes me cough.

Here comes another one. A child looks out at me, points. Oh, please, stop. Let me go with you. I'll be good. I just want to love you. Please. Please. Take me home with you. I won't beg to go inside. Not even when the snow comes. I'll love you. I'll give you kisses. I won't beg.

They go on.

Another car. I trot to meet it. It slows, pulls almost into the ditch. I run to the car, sit and wag my tail. Please. I'm scared. All these cars. Please take me. I'm little. I don't eat much. I'll learn what you want. Please. Please. Please.

He stands on his back legs and waves.

A man looks out. He shakes his head and drives on.

The dog sits at the edge of the road. A truck speeds toward him, a boy hanging half out the window. He yells, laughing, pointing.

I jump up and down and wag my tail. He wants me.

The truck tire comes right at me.

Pain.

Nothing.

MIDNIGHT IN THE MARRIAGE

She: Hey. Turn over.
He: What?
I said turn over.
Why?
You're snoring.
I don't snore.
You always say that.
Yeah? Well, you snore.
You were too snoring and woke me up.
You just woke me up. You musta woke yourself up snoring.
No, you woke me up. I don't snore.
Just go back to sleep, will ya?
Okay. Just turn over.
I'm comfortable. I don't want to move.
Well okay then. Just don't snore.
You know I don't snore.
(Sigh). Just go back to sleep.
You too.
(Silence. Snoring.)
He: Hey, wake up and turn over.
What?
Turn over.
Why?
You're snoring.
Oh, just go to sleep.
I can't. You sound like a freight train.
Freight train? I don't hear a freight train. Is it a tornado?
No, it's you.
What's me?
The snoring.
No, you snore. I don't.
Okay. Just go to sleep.
(Silence. Snoring. Sound of fist smashing pillow.)
He: (Whisper) Please, dear God, just one night let me sleep.
Whatcha say?

I was praying.
This time of night? It must be midnight. Go to sleep.
I can't sleep.
Why? Whatcha asking God to forgive you for?
Just to let me sleep.
What have you done? You been sneaking around?
(Whisper) Oh, dear God. **(Aloud)** You know better.
Then what've you done that you got to ask God to forgive you for?
I'm not asking God to forgive me but to let me go to sleep.
Well, then, hush up and go to sleep.
I can't. You keep snoring.
What? I told you I don't snore.
Okay. You don't snore. It must be a freight train.
You said that before. I don't hear a train. It doesn't run by here at night.
This one runs all night.
I never heard one at night. When did it start running here?
When I married you.
Well, I've never heard it. Go to sleep. I'm tired.
I can't sleep.
How come? You've been coming home late. Who is she?
Nobody.
You've done something. Praying in the middle of the night.
Oh God.
See. I know it. You keep saying you work late. Who is she?
What do you mean, *who is she*?
It's got to be somebody. You don't want me anymore.
You're nuts. Of course I want you. Even tonight.
Yeah? You didn't say anything.
How could I? I touched you and you flinched away.
You tickled me. You're did that on purpose.
I did not.
Did too. You just wanted me to jump. An excuse.
Where in hell do you get these ideas?
I get 'em from you. Who is she?
There is no *she*.
You mean you're queer. I should-a known.
God deliver me from women.
See. I told you. You just admitted you're queer.
I'm not a damn queer.

Well, come to think of it, you sure spend a lot of time with Bill.

Bill? He's my partner. Of course I spend time with him.

Ah-ha. That's what queers call their lovers. *Partner*.

We're attorneys. We have to prepare for trials.

Yeah. Like I have to have Betty from next door help me fix supper.

Where do you get these ideas?

From you.

No, I think you read too many romance novels.

I have to. There's no romance here anymore.

There would be if you didn't flinch every time I touch you.

I do not flinch. You tickle me. That's not romantic.

Oh God! Please! Just go to sleep!

I've been trying. You keep waking me up with your praying.

I'm just praying that you go to sleep and let me sleep.

I'm not keeping you awake. You keep waking me up.

I love you dearly, darling. But your snoring wakes me up.

(Sigh) Here we go again. I'm getting some water.

(Sound of covers moving, bare feet on floor, walking from room, sigh.)

(Snoring, bare feet approaching)

Honey, I brought you some water.

Huh? Whatsat?

I got you some water.

Why did you wake me up?

I brought you some water. Don't you want it?

No, I just want to sleep.

Okay. Go back to sleep. Love ya.

Love ya too.

(Sound of covers, heavy snoring)

She: Honey, turn over. You're snoring.

THE POACHER AND MISS ELLIE

Ranger Gordon Stevens had been assigned to Tickleboro only two weeks before opening day of deer season and had never been in the county before. He had been warned that poaching deer had reached professional levels in the four years since the state had cut back the wildlife resources budgets and no ranger had been assigned within forty miles of Tickleboro.

He forgot such luxuries as time off to hunt or even to sleep. His cell phones, both the official one and the personal one whose number he had given out to numerous landowners, rang from before dawn until after midnight—and sometimes between.

Miss Ellie had been calm when she detailed her problems and said she understood he was being run ragged, but if he had a few minutes, would he check up on poachers who seemed to come onto her place every day.

When she rode with him down the road to show him where the culprits entered her pasture, he saw why. The thirty-foot-high bank from the road to her pasture was scarred with a yard-wide trail cut with deer tracks.

Now he sat in a chair, in bushes, a few feet in front of his truck which he had backed into the brush of an old driveway. He had a perfect view of the dirt road alongside Miss Ellie's pasture.

Headlights appeared over the hill. He closed his eyes to keep his night vision, but when the approaching sounds stopped, he squinted and looked. No sign of headlights. The vehicle had stopped. One door slammed and the vehicle moved down the road toward him, headlights still off. It passed him. As it neared the curve, the headlights came back on.

Poacher has landed. Time to go to work.

He strode down the road toward the deer path and at the bank he hauled himself up the softened dirt by gripping saplings. The fence itself was no barrier—the top strand had long ago been broken and poachers had twisted the bottom two together to make crossing easier. Made it not just easier for the deer, but made it an open-door invitation.

He stepped across the fence. Moonlight shimmered on the frost and showed where the poacher had kicked it as he strode across the meadow toward his stand.

He's going to the stand Miss Ellie showed me yesterday.

Gordon did not follow the frost-free trail but moved to his right, into the moonshadows of the woods, and slipped along as the morning began to wake up behind him. Frost crunched beneath his boots. The wind stirred just enough to make it seem the day itself was beginning to breathe.

A crow called. A jay hollered at the approaching dawn. Gordon stopped beside a white oak and leaned on the trunk. *I better wait till it's light enough he can see me as me and not as a deer. I don't want to be dead cause he's stupid.*

Daybreak was Gordon's favorite time of day. He watched the meadow. A small animal trotted across on its way home for the day, only a form in the mist rising from the frost. Fox, he thought. Overhead came several Canada geese, honking their way to Miss Ellie's pond where she kept the grasses on the forty-foot wide banks cut back. *She won't be happy to have a flock of geese messing up her lake yard. Funny how many people hate the geese and are mad at the state for starting the breeding program here. Well, it's time to move out.*

He pulled a blaze-orange vest from his pocket, shook out the net and pulled it on over his head to cover his green uniform and to notify the poacher he was human, not deer.

He covered the twenty yards to the path into the woods and followed it toward the stand overlooking the creek crossing.

Thirty yards away, his boot crunched a stick. The poacher looked toward him.

"Hold on there, Mister. Game warden."

The poacher didn't hold on. He threw his rifle forward and down, scrambled up from his seat, turned, hurried down the dozen board steps, abandoned his firearm, ran parallel to the creek, toward the roadway, and disappeared to Gordon's right.

Gordon pursued.

The poacher was fast, but Gordon gained on him. He was only ten yards behind the culprit when the poacher reached the fence line.

Gordon heard the car and saw the dust rising from their right. The poacher jumped the fence, cleared the bank and met Miss Ellie's truck head on.

THE TWINS AND THE POACHER

Sonny never let Bobby forget that he was the elder brother, maybe by only a half-hour, but that was enough time to make Sonny the older, the one who must always be in control. At twelve, each received his own rifle, a semiautomatic .22 caliber, heavier than their Red Ryder BB guns and much more powerful.

The first deer season of their lives opened two days later, and with no knowledge of deer or hunting, they set out together on opening day to "bag a monster buck like one crossing the road near the big oak."

Although the frost had melted, the late November morning was still cold. Both boys wore wool shirts under their school jackets. Brown work boots showed splotches of mud and manure from the barnyard. Sunlight turned their red-brown hair the color of October dogwood leaves. Their feet rustled the oak and hickory leaves on the woods trail.

A cottontail jumped from its bed in a hollow of vines and leaves as the boys approached. Bobby pulled up his rifle, but the bunny was gone.

"Sorry, Little Brother," Sonny teased. "That-air rabbit's faster than you."

"Yeah, well maybe so, but you didn't even get your rifle up to your shoulder."

A slight breeze loosened leaves that flitted their way down to join those already coloring the ground.

They called themselves hunting as they laughed their way a half mile from the house. A squirrel barked at them. A jay warned the world strangers were approaching. A woodcock darted from the trail as they neared. An unseen chipmunk chattered at them.

"Hey, look," Sonny whispered and pointed. A deer charged from a thicket of haw bushes toward the boys, lunged another direction and flagged his white tail at them as it disappeared. The woods exploded and buckshot ripped through the branches only inches from the boys. Sonny threw himself at Bobby, and both tumbled into the underbrush as Sonny yelled, "Hey, watch where you're shooting!"

"Oh, God, did I hit you?" came an answer some one hundred yards away, partway up the ridge. Behind the voice someone crackled through the leaves and bushes. As he jumped through the last patch of brush and onto the path, he asked, "Are you hurt?"

The stranger wore new camouflage clothing and carried a Browning semi-automatic .12 gauge with heavy detailed engraving on both stock and barrel.

Cordite filled the air.

Sonny rose, pulled his brother up by the arm and brushed himself off. He pointed toward the man's .12 gauge. "I ain't never seen a gun like that-un. Can I see it up close?"

The man shrugged. "Sure." And handed him the shotgun.

Clutching it, Sonny turned it over and seemed to study it. He looked up, his eyes slits, and said, "You better be damn glad we ain't hurt, Buster. If you'd a-hurt my brutha here, I'd a-kilt you. Now you git off-er our land."

"I'm so sorry." He raised his hands. "I'm sorry. I didn't mean any harm. I saw the bushes move and heard steps and saw the deer."

"You got no business here, Mista. This here is our daddy's place, a mile any which-a way you walk. You best git."

"Give me my shotgun," he said, "and I'll be out of here in a jiffy." He reached for it.

Bobby grabbed it from Sonny. "Ain't no way you taking it outta here, Mista. You're not getting another chance to shoot us."

Bobby backed away from the man and gripped the firearm by the stock with his finger inside the trigger guard. He pointed the muzzle at the stranger. "I'll be a-keeping this," he said. "You ought not be shooting at people. You try to take it and you'll be sorry. Anybody shoots at my brother, I had as soon kill him as look at him. Now you git afore I shoot you and tell my pa I thought it was a deer I was shooting at."

For a moment, the man hesitated. It was more than a mile across the land to where he had left his car, and he wasn't sure he could go directly to it. But both boys had taken a firm stance, shoulder to shoulder, one clutching his shotgun, the other now holding two .22s. He slowly backed off.

"I'll go. I'm so sorry about all this. You just keep the shotgun, seeing as I won't be needing it."

"You ever show up around here again, Mista, and I'll tell every-body you tried to kill us. Now git."

The stranger turned and stepped out at a fast walk.

He was twenty yards away when Bobby called, "Oh, Mista?"

The man turned to see the shotgun pointed at his chest.

"What the—?"

Bobby pulled the trigger.

"Didcha see that deer?" he asked Sonny. "I musta missed it. Anyhow, I'm the big brother now."

"Yeah? Whatcha gonna tell Pa?"

"Nothing. He don't need to see this here new gun."

A gust of wind from the west rained red and yellow leaves on the trail and the body. The brothers headed for home and talked only about how to hide the new shotgun from Pa.

THE LIZARD

She chased another lizard as it ran up the foundation of the house and sought to escape along the wall. As usual, the lizard lost the race. It became resident of Terrarium Number 12 and the subject of her camera for several days.

She could not find it identified in any of her books and even sought it online. Her father suggested she post a picture on her Facebook page and on YouTube. Maybe someone who saw the picture could tell her its identity.

Meanwhile, she fed it grasshoppers and kept a pan of water it its cage. At thirteen she had no fear and caught grasshoppers for her lizards and mice for her two snakes.

Two days after she posted the pictures of the new lizard a professor of herpetology called. He asked if he might visit and see the lizard. She said yes, gave him directions and danced through the house to tell her parents a real professor wanted to see her pets.

He arrived three days later, with camera and two colleagues.

"Where is the lizard," he asked. "I think you have found a new species. I've never seen such."

"It died yesterday. I fed it to my snake."

A DREAM IS A DREAM IS A DREAM

William Atkinson slept. And dreamed. Dreamed he was turkey hunting, settled beside a white oak tree just after sunup. He *yelped* like a love-sick hen, and a tom gobbled. Clad in full-body camouflage, a net mask and gloves to hide his white flesh, he held a Remington .12 gauge semi-automatic shotgun.

In the woods stood two decoys, a jake in half strut and a blue-headed hen. The whisper of wind moved them in a slow waltz and turned them back and forth to face each other.

The gobbler sounded off somewhere in the woods. He slipped through the shadows, his head extended as he cataloged what he saw. He exploded into the strutting dance—one foot forward, close his eyes, thrust his body forward as if to show off his beauty to the hen, turn and throw the other foot forward.

The dreamer eased the shotgun up, sighted to the tom's head and pulled the trigger.

The sound jerked him awake and he sat up.

His right shoulder hurt and as he rubbed the soreness, he recalled the dream.

"Must-a been a heck of a dream if it made my shoulder hurt."

He reached to scratch the intense itching on his leg and turned on the bedside light. *A tick. A damn tick. How the hell did I get a tick? I couldn't have gotten it from trimming the hedge yesterday. I showered.*

He got up, went to the bathroom, found tweezers and returned to perch on the side of the bed. He gripped the tick with the tweezers, turned it over onto its back and tugged. It released its grip. He pulled it off and flushed it into the sewer system. *Don't reckon it'll come back up.*

He returned to bed and sleep. And to the dream. He returned to the woods, to the gobbler lying near his decoys. He wondered howcome the gobbler stayed in his strut rather than attack the jake. Howcome he had killed the gobbler when he knew you can't put shotgun pellets through the fluff when it's in full strut. But he slept on in the dream. He laid down the shotgun by the oak and went to pick up his trophy.

"What do you think you're doing here?" a voice said behind him.

He turned to find another hunter, shotgun parallel across his midsection, his body clad in black, his dark facemask hiding his features.

"I'm just hunting."

"In your dreams. This is my hunting land. Nobody else hunts here." The stranger approached. Almost seven feet tall, he looked down on the dreamer, his eyes inches away. The dreamer sensed the sneer behind the face mask and stepped backwards.

The stranger dropped the shotgun and pulled the Bowie knife from the sheath hanging on his belt. "Nobody gets in my dreams. You are dead, mister." He raised the knife overhead.

That's not how you kill somebody. You stab below the ribs and up into the belly to the heart.

He ran. He woke up on his left side, with his legs running.

The next night he had forgotten the nightmare and fell asleep as easily as a baby being rocked in a cradle. The new dream soothed him as he sat in Symphony Hall and listened to a Beethoven concert. His body throbbed with the rhythms of the Fifth. He dreamed he went from the concert to the Varsity. Where else to go after a wonderful concert or a winning football game but for a frosty orange and a chili dog at Atlanta's most prestigious drive-in founded by a fellow who, having been thrown out of Georgia Tech, made his fortune from the Tech students. The dreamer had been one of those Tech students and still thrived on the Varsity food.

But on the way to the Varsity he was delayed by an accident—a Ford pickup like the one he sold last year—F150, blue with an added running board—had plowed into a power pole and the driver killed. He briefly thought *it could have been me*, but arriving at the drive-in, he put the accident behind him. Nothing could darken his mood. Not even the rain, which began while he sat at the Varsity, his window down to hold the service tray. The wind pushed water through the truck window.

When he rose the next morning, he found the key to the Ford on his dresser, together with the ticket stub from the concert. He picked up the key. *I reckon I kept one when I sold the truck. Must have found it last night and the key is the key to why I dreamed about the truck.*

He threw the ticket stub away without a second glance. He thought it was from a concert he attended the week before. He was puzzled about his rain-soaked jacket thrown across the back of a kitchen chair where it had dripped on the floor.

Two nights later, he dreamed he flew to Alaska for the salmon run at the invitation of an Alaskan friend. They hiked with a tour group through a forest on a path deep with mulch that felt like an expensive plush rug beneath his feet. At the river, he stood on a wooden platform built to keep the tourists safe and watched the bears catch salmon. He noticed a man wearing a coat like his own, a man with a camera, a man stupid enough to leave the platform and try to get closer to the bears for pictures.

He turned his attention back to a female bear on the far side of the river. She splashed into the shallows, plunged her head under water and came up with a fish that flapped against both sides of her face. She charged to the distant bank and offered her catch to her cub.

A woman screamed. He spun around. The idiot camera man flailed as a bear attacked. The attack lasted only seconds—the bear clamped his jaws around the man's throat, lifted him, shook him to limpness, dropped the carcass on the bank and returned to fishing. One of two dozen, he was just another bear in the crowd.

"If we are going fishing, let's go. I've seen enough bears," he said to his friend.

He fished from a bank in front of a small cabin. The sun warmed his back, but the wind shifted to the north and intensified. He caught seven fish that totaled almost one hundred pounds. He stayed in the sun but sheltered from the wind while he cleaned and filleted his fish, wrapped them for freezing and boxed them as luggage to fly home.

He was locked in the plane's toilet when the commotion began. Gunfire in the cabin. He trembled with fear that the plane was going to crash or that he would be shot if he opened the door. But a few minutes later, someone knocked on the door. "Hey, it's over. The hijackers are dead."

He returned to his seat to find a passenger there. Dead.

He awoke from his dream, tried to forget the details of bear and hijackers while he prepared coffee. He went to the fridge for cream and found a box of wrapped salmon.

I guess I didn't dream about going to Alaska after all. I did go. I just must be losing my mind to forget something like that.

He took the box of fish to the basement to put into the freezer.

A week later, he dreamed again. Somehow he knew he dreamed and tried to wake up. But the dream gripped him and he couldn't wake. He walked along a path beside the downtown city park and followed the path into the woods. He had never been in those woods but in his dream he knew the pathways.

October colors drifted from the trees and mixed yellows and reds along the ground. The breeze chilled him and in his dream he shivered. In his bed, he shivered.

He reached a stream of slow-moving shallow water that reflected the maple reds and the poplar and hickory yellows. He danced along the pathway and kicked off his shoes to wade in the creek. The water was colder than the wind and the pebbles in the creek bed hurt his feet. He climbed from the water and continued down the pathway, without his shoes.

The sun dashed to the horizon in front of him faster than time. As it sank, the moon rose behind him and threw his blue shadow on the path. He was forced to follow wherever the shadow went.

Snow began to fall, but the moon stayed bright. In his dream he hurried to get inside somewhere, to escape the cold.

The snow ended and a rainbow circled the sky above him. Somewhere in the night someone laughed. Not a pleasant laugh, but the laughter of delight over something evil. Fear rose in him. He tried to retreat, but his shadow pulled him forward, toward the laughter.

A man materialized from the darkness. No sound of footsteps or rustle of clothing. Clad in black, he held a knife. The knife looked familiar. A hunting knife. A Bowie knife. A knife a hunter would use to butcher a deer—or clean a turkey. Or to gut an enemy in a fight to the death at the Alamo.

The man grinned. "Time you got here. You've been holding off too long. You were supposed to die on that turkey hunt."

In his dream he knew he would wake before the man caught him. No one died in a dream. He turned to run.

The man grabbed his shoulder and spun him around. The knife reflected moonlight as it rose from below his waist, plunged into his belly and penetrated his chest.

He awoke, sat up, saw the knife, yanked it out. Blood spurted and soaked the mattress.

I just woke up dead. But if I'm dead how did I wake up?

The obituary the next day read:

William Atkinson died peacefully in his sleep last night.

Second Place, Vega Award for Speculative fiction

THE OLD MAN BY THE ROAD

I found a new way to go from the family home to the town where I worked. It cut three miles and several minutes off the drive. That is, until I began stopping at the old man's truck to pick out fruit and veggies to take home—to my apartment when I headed north, and Fridays to pick up items for my mom when going south and home to Tickleboro.

His supplies varied by seasons. Early July he had watermelons, and when I stopped to purchase one for me and one for one of my co-workers, I commented, "My dad always said watermelons weren't any good until July 4th. His parents wouldn't pick their own melons until Independence Day."

He nodded, raised his battered straw hat, scratched his head and said, "Just what my grandparents always said too. I had a couple of Yankees here last week and they shore did insist I pick them some. I had to tell them to stop by when they were going t'other way. I don't pick 'em till July fourth either."

The next time I stopped, he had tomatoes galore on the tailgate. Looked like the baskets and buckets-full we picked when I was a youngster and Mother and my Aunt Eugenia canned gallons on a weekend. I asked if a basket I couldn't see into held cucumbers and he said, No, it was full of squash.

"Just what I want," I replied. "Let me have a dozen. It's my favorite veggie. I'll cook them with onions for supper and have chicken salad with it. Can't beat that for a summer supper."

Before summer was over, I stayed around to chat on every stop. He asked me what I did in the country, why I didn't have a garden of my own. I explained I worked five days in Atlanta and couldn't find time on the weekends to work a garden in the country.

"Got yourself a real farm?" he asked.

"Yes. Big enough for the bootleggers to keep a still going half the time, especially since I can't get over all the land ever weekend."

He laughed, not just with a smile but with a glimmer in his eyes. "Lawd-a-mercy, I remember when I was in my teens I thought the only good way to earn money was to moonshine. I helped ole Billy Stykes with his still." He pointed down the hill toward the big creek. "We ran about a hundred gallons a week for almost a year. Right down yonder, on Rocky Branch. Never did get caught, but my pa found out what I was doing and he whupped me good. Told me to make an honest living. And from that day on, I was either in school or walking behind the plow horse."

"Sounds like your pa was a good man. And taught you how to have a good crop."

"That he did. But come fall and muscadines, he taught me how to make wine. He had a crock that'd hold about ten gallons of grapes. He wouldn't let me taste it till I was old enough to get drafted."

"You in the army?"

"No. I joined the Marines before I got drafted. Got lucky, too. I was in between Korea and Vietnam. Never had to shoot anybody and never got shot at. But I was the best shot in my company." He grinned and nodded three times.

"You were?"

"That I was. I learned to shoot when I was just a little tyke, shooting squirrels with a .22 single-shot rifle when fall came and I didn't have to plow."

Every stop I learned a little more about this gentleman. Sometimes the stories reminded me of my father—Dad had made muscadine wine. Like the old man he had run a tube from the fermenting bottle into a pan of water to keep air out and let the fermentation gases escape. But Dad didn't always keep the water deep enough for the end of the tube to stay under, so when air could slither up the tube, instead of wine, he brewed vinegar.

Like my father, the old man smoked a pipe, at least I think he smoked it. I never saw it lit, but he would clench it between his teeth and remove it to talk, most of the time. Sometimes he just talked around it.

Dad wore glasses to read, and this old man perched his on the end of his nose when he wrote my charges on a paper bag and tallied the figures. I thought it funny that like Dad's his glasses were minus one of the ear supports.

Every trip was a new discovery. He had apples and muscadines in September and October, and pickled cucumbers in winter. And stories about his life. His son was off in the Marines. His grandson and daughter-in-law lived out in California and he dreamed about maybe one day flying out to visit, but he reckoned he might be too old to fly.

"I ain't got my angel wings yet," he laughed. "Maybe when I get a pair I can fly out to see them."

He rose from the cane-bottom pine chair and stepped to the cab of the pickup. He returned with a bottle of muscadine wine. He said, "You stop by here at least four times a month. It's time for me to say thank you. This here is wine I made last year. It's best I ever made. I want you to have this."

"Oh, I couldn't do that. This is your living. But I tell you what. I write books. That's my living. I'll swap you a book for the wine." I went to the car, slipped the book into a small paper sack I used when I held book signings. It was my novel about country life some forty years before. He'd enjoy the chapter about the judge's daughter going on a liquor still raid and the main character getting sprayed by a skunk on a possum hunt.

The next weekend, I looked forward to seeing that white oak tree and his long-bed faded-red pickup pulled under it and to hear what he thought about my novel. But it wasn't there the Friday before Labor Day as I went south. I figured he was taking time off for the holiday, and just kept on going south.

But a week later, there was still no truck there.

I stopped, pulled into the driveway across the road, to the small clapboard farmhouse. Smoke rose from the chimney. I hesitated and then knocked on the door.

A stooped, white-haired lady opened it. She wore a cotton house dress with a hand-knitted sweater. The fireplace warmed the house and its smoke smelled like home to me.

"I'm sorry to bother you," I said, "but I missed the gentleman under the oak. I wanted to get some more of his pickled cukes."

Tears welled up but she tried to blink them away.

"He was my younger brother, but he died the Tuesday before Labor Day. I miss him so much. You must be the lady he talked about. You never just drove on by. You always stopped to buy something or to say hello. He liked you a lot. But you never told him your name. You're the lady who wrote that book."

"I never thought about names," I said. "Yes, I'm Candace Harcourt. He became a friend. I am so sorry for your loss. I feel the loss too. It'll never be the same for me to drive by here."

She pulled her head up higher and frowned. "Harcourt is really your name? Your name or your husband's name?"

"It's mine," I said. "Not married, at least not yet."

"You any kin to William Cantrell Harcourt, founder of Tickleboro about a hundred years ago?"

"Why, yes, he was my great-great-grandfather. Why?"

She smiled. "Well, I be darned. No wonder you two got along so good. Old Cantrell was our great-great-grandpappy too. Com'on in. I got his portrait hanging in the sitting room. Let's us visit."

THE CRIPPLE AND THE POACHERS

Bonnie had not hunted since she broke her leg two years ago. Unfortunately, word had gotten around town that she was on crutches. Poaching had increased. But this year, she planned to hunt, poachers be damned if they came around.

Days on crutches were behind her. She might need a cane to get across rough ground on her way to her stand, but a ground blind would be easy, and in the meadow's edge, she could spot any approaching poacher. By next year, she'd be on her climbing stand again anyway.

Carl and Kenny, her two hunting buddies, came from Athens to help out on Labor Day weekend as they did every year. Today, they were working on her blind to overlook the food plot. Tomorrow, they would plow and seed the land, and if time allowed and the weather man promised rain, they would spread fertilizer on Monday.

The sun only peeked at them all Saturday morning through clouds that scooted overhead in front of a strong Gulf wind. Their black bottoms threatened rain that did not fall.

For her blind, she selected a spot behind the large sweet gum on the edge of the field, the one that still had barbed wire running through it from the days her family ran cattle. The wire would be perfect to weave pine branches into, and she would hang a solid camouflage cloth behind it to break up her pattern. She would duplicate the setup behind her chair.

She would be able to look over the large white oak midfield where the buck of a lifetime had been seen. She wondered if the reports of that buck were only neighborhood fables. She had killed her last buck while he fed under that oak tree three years ago. Was the one everybody talked about his son?

In her climbing stand that year, she was in a pine only ten yards behind the sweetgum. This year, she would still face northeast, toward the dirt road the buck had been seen to cross to reach her meadow. Best of all, she would also overlook the persimmon tree that began to bear last fall. From her kitchen window she had seen deer in her yard run from one persimmon to another to try to beat the others to the treat. They would surely be under this one too.

Not much of a meadow now. But it will be when I get this trash cut and the field overseeded with clover and rye. It won't pull the deer in till after the persimmons are gone.

"Hey, Bonnie, look here," Carl called from the edge of the woods where he stood with limb cutters. "Here's a blind. It looks like it was just put here."

She limped the fifty yards to a clump of bushes. Sure enough, a ground blind. An expensive blind, a tent with viewing windows on three side and an entrance on the fourth. Around the tent the poachers had draped a layer of heavier camouflage and over that hung a layer of leafy camouflage. It blended in so well with the surrounding bushes that Carl had not seen it until he was only a few feet away.

"They saw the deer crossing," she said. Mentally, she pictured the path torn by deer hooves for several years. Anyone looking for deer signs, for anything to clue them in for a place to poach, could not miss the paths. Nor could they miss seeing the break in the fence. She shook her head at the idea of having to poacher hunt on opening day. Her first opening day in two years, but they seemed a lifetime. She turned her attention back to the blind.

She located the loop holding the double layers of camouflage and pulled the cover back. She stepped inside, unfolded the chair and sat. She had a perfect view to the right, to the oak tree. *But they can't see the persimmon.* She stood up, refolded the chair and stepped out of the blind

"I think they haven't been in here before. Unless they have another hidey-hole. Let's look around."

She followed the edge of the meadow to the southwest while Carl crossed to the other side to check that edge. Kenny dropped over the ridge to scout the creek. Bonnie and Carl met at the four-wheeler trail on the far side of the meadow and followed it.

"There," Carl said. "It's got to be close by. That's the path leading to the persimmons at the creek."

Kenny came up from the creek. "I found it. Just far enough off the trail so you couldn't see where it overlooks the creek crossing and the persimmons down in the bottom."

They went to the creek. Like the first one, that blind was a combination of tent and several layers of camouflage.

"Let's break this one down," she said. "They won't be here before opening day. I'll head them off when they get here. Probably have a wife drop them off and they'll come in on the same the trail the deer use. Cross the fence where the two top strands are broken. I'll be poacher hunting on opening day."

It was three weeks off, so she went ahead with her usual plans, bushhogged the meadow and overseeded it as a food plot. This year, however, she left the upper half, toward the public road, grown up and unseeded. "Give the deer some protection from the poachers on the road."

With no ranger in her county these days, it would be up to her to catch the poachers. She told Carl and Kenny they were to go deer hunting. She would poacher hunt and call the sheriff on her cell phone when she had them.

Opening day, a half-hour before first light, she was dressed in full camouflage, even with a face mask, and settled in the poacher's chair which she relocated behind the blind. Her loaded .12 gauge lay across her knees. Day was breaking when she heard the car stop, two doors slam, and knew she faced at least two, if not three, poachers. The car left.

Bushes alongside the road rustled as the poachers worked their way through. Moments later, she heard them whispering. Two, she figured.

The eastern sky had brightened enough that the world seemed flooded with the light of a full moon. Day was marching in.

"I'll see ya. Good luck. Be careful and don't get caught," one said.

Laughter. "No way. That old cripple won't be anywhere around here. All she does is have those hired men plant for the deer. She can't do anything herself."

She rose from behind the blind, and with her shotgun held cross-ways, she walked around it.

"This old crip is putting you both under arrest for trespassing and for hunting without permission," she said. "Take those rifles off your shoulders and lay them on the ground."

Neither man moved.

"Like I said, men, lay your rifles on the ground."

"She's not gonna shoot us," the shorter one said.

"I wouldn't bet on it, Mister. This is loaded with double ought and it'll lay you both out with one pull of the trigger. I might not be pointing it at you this second, but I will shoot if you give me cause. I've been shot at by the likes of you before."

Her range was perfect to spread the shot to both men. "And there won't be anybody around to say you didn't try to shoot me. Now, how about you lay the rifles down."

She kept the business end of the shotgun pointed slightly to her left. The two men stood in front of her.

She stepped closer.

The taller man, to her right, reached for the shoulder strap. "Real slow-like. You first," she nodded to him.

She turned her attention away from the shorter man on her left for a moment.

He grabbed his rifle off his shoulder. As he turned it toward her, she caught the movement and spun her shotgun toward him. Her shotgun barrel smacked into his arm and pushed the business end of his 30.06 toward his buddy.

Both firearms discharged.

She pulled out her cell phone and dialed 911. When the dispatcher answered, she asked for the sheriff, who immediately came on line.

"Morning, Bill. I need one of your guys out here. And maybe you too. Got me two poachers."

"I'll send somebody out to take them in."

"I think you better come along. And send the undertaker for both."

JONATHAN'S CAVE

For three days after his two buddies had given up and gone home, he had walked over rocks, slid down gulches, driven his off-road four-wheeler where the land was passable, and scrabbled up shale hillsides in the blistering August heat to check shadows and illusions on what seemed like a thousand cliffs in search of the cave.

He stared at another illusion, a darkness beside brush near the top of the ridge where sunlight seemed to vanish into the shadows. Was that the cave? He lifted the binoculars, tugged his cap brim down to shade his eyes and studied the rocks and brush..

"Damn if I ain't found it," he muttered. "That's gotta be it."

He lifted his backpack from atop the cooler strapped on the rear rack of the Honda FourTrax and checked its contents. Two full bottles of water, three packs of dried food, flashlight, spare batteries and the large spool of twine he referred to as his bread crumbs to mark his trail in and out when he found the cave.

He rummaged into the cooler and pulled out two bottles of water. *Reckon I can't stay but maybe tonight and tomorrow seeing this just leaves me three bottles of water and two wraps of dried beef to get home on. I'll just look around a bit and flag the bushes up yonder. I'll come back soon's I restock and can map it real good. I can spend the night here and head out in the morning.*

Studying the sleeping bag strapped to the front rack of the four-wheeler, he decided to leave it. If night caught him at the cave, one night on the rock floor was not going to cripple him and it was just extra weight to tote right now. It would not be the first night he had used the backpack for a pillow.

He checked to be sure the roll of surveyor's tape was still in the front pocket of the pack. He had carried the tape for three years in his search for this cave. Now he would use it—flag the cave entrance today and flag his way out of the mountains tomorrow.

Won't need no flagging to get my name on this here mountain and this here cave neither. I'm gonna name it for me, Jonathan's Mountain and Jonathan's Cave. Fix up the map too when I start outta here.

Jonathan shook his head and smiled as he swung the backpack onto his shoulders. Every since the old man had told his father about the cave, hinted it held a treasure beyond words and left for one more trip to the cave, Jonathan and his father had talked of finding the cave. And maybe the old man's bones, for he never returned from that last visit to his treasure.

The old man left neither directions nor map. Only the comment that it was close. And now Jonathan anticipated the treasure and the fame it would bring him.

I'll hafta find that picture of me back when I was in the army. I didn't look so old then, hadn't turned old-looking like a cowboy in the sun too much. And hadn't had to have half my nose cut off from the cancer. They can put that old picture in the paper.

He studied the mountainside, but saw no sign of a trail. *Oh, well, I'll make myself a path.* He strode to the base of the cliff, stepped around large boulders and began the climb. He walked a few yards, but as the shale slipped down under his feet, he turned sideways and crab-stepped upward. At times, he held onto boulders to keep his feet and to haul himself upward.

Sweat poured down his back and dripped off his chin. After an hour, he stopped to rest, wiped his face on his sleeves and drank heavily from one bottle of water. *Gotta go easy on this. Not but half-way up my mountain and about to drink up half a bottle. Yeah. My mountain. My cave.*

A hundred years from now, everyone would call it "Jonathan's Cave," not the "lost cave" that an old man had talked about more than twenty years ago. They'd put his picture at the cave entrance, too.

He climbed onward, at times on hands and knees to get over larger boulders, at times walking slantwise across the rocks rather than straight up and sometimes pulling himself forward by limbs of one of the trees scattered among the rocks. He was not even half-way to the cave mouth when he realized it would be dark by the time he reached the entrance.

"Night ain't a problem," he said to the mountain, "you're mine now."

He halted, swung his back pack onto a flat rock and perched on the rock's edge to catch his breath. He pulled off his baseball cap, wiped sweat from his face with his forearm and snugged the cap back down over his black hair. He pulled the half-empty bottle of water out of the backpack and emptied it in two long swallows. He wedged the empty bottle between two rocks. *I'll mark the trail.*

After a half-hour's rest, he began climbing again. When he stood in the opening, the sun had crept below the mountains and the moon had not come up. In the afterglow of sundown, the cave mouth gaped open to forever's darkness.

He gathered downfall for firewood and set up camp about ten feet inside the entrance before night replaced the last of the evening. To save batteries, he found his way around the entrance by light from the campfire and counted three tunnels leading away. He decided to wait until morning, when he'd be more rested, to explore further.

Supper of dried beef and water over, he pulled off his boots, stretched out on his back, pushed the edge of the backpack under his neck and tried to sleep. His mind would not shut down but twisted his body from side to side with his excitement. He watched the moon rise outside the cave and spread blue shadows over the night. The moon passed over the mountain before he fell asleep.

Violent shivers woke him to cold and pain deep in his back; even his hands and toes felt as if they were packed in ice. He reached for the cover of his sleeping bag before he remembered he did not bring it up the mountain. His hand touched damp stone.

He sat up, wrapped his arms across his chest for warmth and looked into darkness. No embers from last night's fire. No light patch at the cave opening.

Only wetness. And cold. Water glued his clothes to his back and legs. He was in a puddle. *Musta rained last night.*

Oh my gawd, the water's moving. I'm in a creek. How in hell did I get in a creek?

He started to rise, but his legs, stiff from the cold, didn't want his weight. He rolled onto his knees and crawled out of the water. He sat and pulled his knees up so he could reach his feet. Colder than his hands. He wrapped his fingers over his toes to relieve some of the cold pain and to squeeze some water out of his socks.

The cave. He was in *the* cave. Adrenalin flooded him and he scrambled to his feet. The flashlight. Where had he left it? Beside his boots? Stuck in one of his boots? *Where in hell are my boots? Where in hell is my backpack?*

Jonathan patted the stone around himself. Nothing but moisture and rock. He began to pat himself down, first one pocket and then another. Nothing in the side pockets. He remembering empting them when he took out his knife to shave kindling for the fire.

A whisper of movement grabbed his thoughts, and he ducked to the side. Another whisper, and the air seemed to flood with the wings of bats. No strong odor of bats or bat droppings, so these had come from deep inside somewhere. Or were they coming home before sunrise?

He shivered at the thought and reached into his cargo pockets. There was the small flashlight he always kept as a back up to the heavy duty light. His tin of kitchen matches was there too, still closed tight against the water.

He clicked on the flash and got only a faint glow. "You gotta last me," he said and stepped forward. He kicked something with his toe and yelped. His voice came back to him from different directions. He gritted his teeth. The cold made the pain worse.

He pointed the light down and saw he had stumped his toes on sticks dumped into a pile as if someone had been preparing for a fire. Most had been broken into short pieces ready to burn; several limbs lay off to the side, still unbroken.

"Long enough to be torches." His whisper echoed back to him. Nearby was the ash pile from someone's fire. "Thanks, Old Man. You sure have saved me with those sticks."

With the batteries of the flash weakening, he needed a torch. Why had he been so careless about backup batteries for the little light?

He reached into his pocket for the tin of kitchen matches, removed one and struck it with his thumb nail. The flame bit his fingers before he got the limb to burn. He tried a second match, tilted the limb so it pointed downward and the match had more fuel, and in a moment the torch blazed. When he moved, weird shadows danced over the rocks and made everything seem to be in constant motion.

Only silence spoke to him. Not even the stream trickled. No bats flitted by. He turned around to look for something familiar. He lifted the stick higher and turned another slow circle. Only darkness beyond the light. He began to walk, he thought in the direction the bats had come from, the direction that would lead him out.

As he neared the wall, he saw two tunnels about six feet apart. Something was wrong. The three tunnels he remembered from last night were at least twenty feet apart, not this close. He rubbed the burning end of the stick against the stone at the opening of the right-hand tunnel to mark it with soot and began a slow circle around the chamber.

Seven openings.

He leaned his shoulder against the soot mark. Maybe he could follow the bats out—or in. Which way were they going? He looked at his watch. It was after eight. But morning or night? Were the bats coming in or going out? Surely they were coming in—he wouldn't have slept around the clock.

His gut knotted. What difference would anything make—the bats in, or the bats out, or even which tunnel he took. He was here to stay. Forever. They would for sure call it *Jonathan's Cave*, for he'd never retrace the steps he had taken while sleepwalking.

Honorable Mention: (as "The Cave Walker") The George T. Youngblood Short Fiction Award, Southeastern Writers Association, 2010

THE ELK PHOTOGRAPHER

The smell of frying food assaulted Jessica as she entered the café, but as she turned to seek a table, a photograph claimed her attention. It did not hang on the wall of the eatery but on a wall through an open door. She followed her gaze into the gallery where she stood before the photograph and stared in awe.

Two bull elk clashed antlers; several does stood beyond them as if they were entranced by the battle for their affection. The photograph glowed with rays of golden mist rising as the setting sun sneaked streams of light between trees.

"Oh gawd, I'd die for a photograph like that," she muttered.

"You needn't die for it," a male voice said.

She turned to the man leaning back in an executive chair behind a desk. "You took this?" she asked.

"I took that down near Cherokee, but we have a lot of elk around here. Go up to the lodge at Broken Antler Park and the ranger can let you know where the elk are feeding now. Best time to see them in the fields is the first two hours of daylight and the last two hours before dark."

She didn't bother with lunch, but headed for the Broken Antler Ranger station for information. And spent the next two days and more than 300 miles on twisting, curving, dangerous dirt roads to find an elk. Just one elk. Or even one bear would do. Maybe a whitetail buck. Everybody she talked to said this was the area for wildlife—Eastern Kentucky, where the Elk Restoration Project had released collared elk years ago. Long enough ago that now hunters gambled for permits to hunt the giant deer of the eastern United States.

But where in the heck were the critters? She had been to two of the sites labeled "elk viewing" on the list of ten sites the ranger recommended. No sign of an elk. At the first site, all she had seen was a frog. *A frog, can you imagine a frog on a mountain side, hopping along a gravel and dirt road?*

On the road to the second site, three wild turkey hens had stepped out of the brush, spun around several times as if undecided where to go when they spotted her approaching car. *Well, at least this site produced something. Six birds, if you count the two crows and the buzzard.*

Day three, she slept late and waited for the afternoon to be half gone before she headed out again. *No point in sitting in the sun for five hours. I'll get to this site about an hour before sundown. Won't be a crowd there anyhow.*

She thought back to the first site, two days ago. A flat mountain top with a 360-degree view. Timber on two-thirds of the view, but the other side, facing the setting sun, showed a white truck parked along a rough dirt road and several horses grazing in the distance. *White, the color for all wildlife to flee. Won't be a deer of any kind in sight.*

After two hours of glassing the area, she had spotted two people and a roaming dog approach the truck. All three climbed aboard, the dog in the truck bed, his head hanging over the side. The vehicle drove off down the dirt road. Disgusted, and knowing no member of the deer family would be in the area, she had left.

Last night, she had taken the ranger's advice and headed to what was considered the Number Two spot to see elk. He had said the Number One spot was a large field that was hosting a musical event and would be so crowded with people no elk would show. Give that spot a rest. So today, she was off to the number three spot.

The ranger had given her detailed directions: Pass the town, turn off onto the Boy Scout Camp Road and follow it through two towns, to the second Boy Scout Camp sign and turn across the bridge to the right. Took her two hours to reach the bridge and another twisting, turning, dangerous road, with the locals speeding toward her or tailgating so close she pulled off several times to let them speed by.

Across the bridge, she entered another rough, unpaved road. Worse than the curves were the rocks and potholes—rocks big enough to bottom out the oil pan and potholes deep enough that only her shoulder harness kept her from bouncing into the roof of her Subaru Outback.

On and on the road went. Finally, she saw the third sign for the scout camp, where she was to go uphill to the viewing area. She stopped and looked the entrance over. *I wouldn't take my old farm Jeep up that road.*

She drove straight ahead with hope. Over a low ridge, across more rocks, dust rising behind her even at ten miles per hour, wind whipping the grass. *No deer in its right mind is going to be out in a field with this wind.* Another half-mile and she reached another road leading up to the mesa.

Looks bad, but not as bad as the other one. I'll give it a go.

She started up the road, but after forty yards, she gave up. Potholes. More rocks. Russian olive trees brushed against both sides of the car.

I'm gonna ruin my new Outback if I go up there. And there's no cell phone reception. I could be stuck here. And have to walk out. No way I'm going up there.

She mentally thanked the salesman for insisting she get the Outback with the safety features instead of the 2008 used vehicle she looked at. The used one had less than 100,000 miles and was spick and span. Not a scratch, inside sparkling, had belonged to only one owner, an old lady who drove it to her country estate and back to Atlanta. This one, however, had a backup camera the '08 did not have. She backed up without turning her head, just watched the camera image on the dashboard screen. The camera even showed the location of the largest rocks, the ones that could bust a tire and leave her stranded.

Now it was day three and she had driven another seventy miles to reach this site, the Number One elk viewing site in the state—at least the ranger promised. It was elk season, and an empty truck stood at the edge of the field, beneath an oak. It motivated her to slip on her red vest. The area looked promising; at least the truck was black, not white. No other people stood around to scare off the wildlife. No kids galloping around and screaming.

She unloaded tripod, Nikon camera, lens case and chair and attached the 600-mm, f 2.4 lens to the tripod, adjusted its height for her to be standing to shoot. After she attached the camera to the lens, she settled into her chair.

An hour passed. She almost dozed, but the roar of an approaching truck brought her back to full wakefulness.

The truck stopped beside her car and a couple got out, each one holding binoculars.

"Seeing anything?" The woman asked.

"Nothing. This is my third day, and still nothing."

"We come here almost every day. That damn musical event scared everything off. I hope it's been enough time for them to come back this afternoon."

"I hope so too. How jumpy are the elk here? You know, with hunting season just opened?"

"It hasn't seemed to bother the ones that feed here. That's a fancy camera setup you got there."

"Yeah, I bought it special for this trip. Cost me an arm and a leg."

"All we got is our binocs to bring them in close. But we can get a good view here. And this here phone camera done good for us the other day. Let me show you." The stranger pulled her phone from the back pocket of her jeans and turned it on. As she walked toward Jessica, she ran her finger down the pictures. "This here one I got two days afore the music event."

"Be gosh, he was right up to you. Why, I'd die to get that good a picture."

"He shore was close. You ain't gonna hafta die for some spectacular pictures. But you shore ain't gonna get no pictures worth dying for with that-air getup lessen it be good enough to take pictures when it's about dark. Them elks'll be along about another half-hour or hour. That camera any account when it gets late?"

"Some. I can adjust it for twilight."

"We don't ever stay here that late. It gets too dark for my phone camera."

The strangers walked away and Jessica settled back to wait. An hour passed, and the couple waved goodbye and drove off.

The late afternoon wind chilled her. Jessica went to her SUV for her camouflage jacket. She shook out the folds and donned it, giving no thought to the picture of the bull elk's forequarters and head on the back.

Another quarter-hour and the elk appeared. Two bulls and several cows. She began snapping pictures. The herd moved toward her. One bull bugled and charged the other.

She held down the button on *continuous* and captured the threatening approach, the battle and the younger bull's flight. The larger bull bugled his triumph. And bred two of the cows. Her hands shook with excitement.

When the bull began to feed, she reviewed the pictures. "My God, what a series. Like I said, this is good enough to die for."

She stood up and stretched. She did not hear the shot and the Remington 30.06 Core-Lokt® bullet exploded through her back and heart so rapidly she was dead before she fell.

ASHES TO ASHES

I keep my eyes shut and see splotches of darkness. Rorschach patterns dance against my eyelids and float from darkness to patches of light and to a background of sandstorms. I am going to sleep—not just for the night, but for forever. The dark shapes float like clouds ready to explode into a tornado. But I feel only peace as the darkness deepens and I drift into the distance.

I am ashes now, just as I had asked. But locked into a jug. I don't like being locked into a jug. I asked to be scattered among my daffodils *beside the lake, beneath the trees.*

Ahhh, they listened! I am floating on the breeze, drifting down, down, down and the daffodils are blooming. I can rest now and see everything from here, see the world as it travels around the sun forever, and forever see what happens here beside my lake.

There is no time. This moment is yesterday, tomorrow and forever.

Someone comes to plant more daffodil bulbs. He is young, a face I do not know. Perhaps he is a cousin or has the land been sold and this is a new owner? The flowers erupt in color and blanket the bank. The boy is gone. An old man, stooped and wrinkled, carrying the face of the boy, picks flowers and carefully separates them by strength. *He knows* how different daffodils kill off others and will separate them for the moment. But that moment is gone now.

Persimmons splat onto the ground and whitetail deer run to the lake bank to compete for the fruit. Oh, how I remember the time I ate a green one and it turned my mouth inside out. But the deer don't seem to care that frost has not fallen on these.

A coyote—no, a wolf! There were no wolves here in my days of walking this land. But the wolf carries a deer haunch as it trots through the thickets alongside the lake bank. The lake has gone into somewhere in the past, the bed now filled with erosion and cattails. And snakes, dragonflies and red-winged blackbirds live where once I fished for bass and bream. A green heron wades in the muck and vanishes into the past.

But there is no past and no future, only the moment. The earth turns. Rains come, flood the land and wash the trash and junk out of the pond. An alligator makes her home here with me and hatches out her brood—or is it a thousand broods as bull gators call for love and silence again falls on the land

Elk come, push each other across the meadow nearby and bugle their way into the future—or to the past. Oh, how I loved to photograph them and hear them call across the fields and hills. But they are gone again as quickly as the flash of lightning against a summer thunderhead.

The earth trembles. Animals flee. Wind floods darkness from the west. Debris blackens the sky like migrating blackbirds. Yellowstone's caldera sends its ashes to join me. She colors sunrise and sunset. Elk no longer flee the wolf. Gators no longer bellow. Owls no longer welcome the night, for night will not end or begin again.

There is no tomorrow, no yesterday and no forever. Nothing exists except the now and ashes.

THE KID AND THE TURKEY

He knew at fourteen he would be illegal, out in the woods alone with his .12 gauge. State law demanded he always be in sight of an adult. *Yeah, right, one of the two adults back at camp, snoring, sleeping off their four-beer lunch. Lots of good either one would do as a supervisor on a turkey hunt.*

The kid knew where to go and how to hunt. After all day yesterday with his father and this morning with Uncle Sammy and weeks of practicing his turkey calls he decided he could go it alone. *Let them sleep it off. I'm gonna go get me a turkey.*

This morning on the hardwood ridge, he had seen the ground mulch torn up with turkey scratching. So fresh the smell of the damp earth stayed in his nostrils long after he and his father had left. If the birds weren't feeding there this morning, he was sure they would be back this afternoon, back for the acorns remaining from last fall. Fresh droppings of both tom and hen splotched the area. By mid-afternoon, the birds would be feeding, not courting. He wouldn't even need to use a call.

All he had to do was go to the oak ridge and wait. Hunker down and blend into the trees and bushes, and along would come the birds.

It was a good half-mile from the camp to the ridge. He couldn't picture the area but knew there was one tree he wanted at his back. He packed a bottle of water, a snack bar and his leafy camouflage outfit. Dressed in his lightweight camouflage and carrying his new Remington semi-automatic .12 gauge, he headed for the ridge.

His long strides covered the distance easily. Twice he stopped to be sure the loaded shotgun was on safety. He didn't want to stumble and shoot himself in the foot with his Number 2 birdshot. He grinned at the thought.

One of his high school buds had done just that last spring, propped his shotgun snout on his foot and forgot it was loaded. Pulled the trigger, shot off his foot and now would be unable to hunt or play basketball. He shook his head at the thought—his friend had planned on a basketball scholarship for college and now had nothing.

Leastways, I've got better sense.

As he crossed the soggy meadow, a deer snorted. He stopped to watch the white tail wave goodbye. Next fall, he was going to deer hunt. He had asked for a deer rifle for his birthday this year. The shotgun came for last Christmas. He had saved up his lawn care money to buy the camouflage outfit.

He stopped halfway up the side of the oak ridge to listen. Leaves rustled. He closed his eyes to concentrate on the pattern. Not a "scratch, scratch/scratch," the three-part scratch pattern of the turkey. More of a "hop-hop/hop." *A squirrel.*

He eased up the ridge, took one step, listened, then two steps and looked and listened. Only the squirrel—he spotted it, a fox squirrel, gray with a black head. At the ridge top, he looked around for the tree he had wanted to use this morning, but Pa had insisted they sit by a sweetgum with a bush beside it. And there had been no way for him to move his shotgun without slamming it into the bush.

Not gonna sit there again.

An oak wide enough to hide his narrow body had a natural swale in the trunk that would provide a back rest curved to fit his spine. The kid kicked out a spot to sit so that his back fit into the trunk and his bottom fit neatly into the swale he kicked out.

He pulled the leafy camouflage out of his pack, slid it over his head and stuck his arms through the sleeves. He sat, drew both knees up and draped the material over his legs. Should any turkey look at him it would see only a pile of leaves. He nestled the butt of the shotgun up to his shoulder and rested the stock on his knee.

He waited and listened.

Something rustled the leaves to his left and he cut his eyes in that direction. A deer tiptoed toward him. She searched for last fall's acorns for a good half-hour, alone. Every few minutes, she lifted her head and looked around. Twice he thought she detected him, but she continued to browse.

Bored, he rested his chin on his knees and watched her. *She sure has got a big belly. Looks like she's gonna have twins. I bet this is gonna be a good place to doe hunt this fall. If I get that rifle for my birthday.*

The doe lifted her head, stomped one front hoof and stared beyond him, off to his left. She moved her head slightly side to side.

She's spotted something. He heard the soft chatter of turkeys and the rustle of dry leaves as they approached. Still out of his sight, they began to scratch for whatever acorns remained.

He had been told a turkey could see human eyes blink from a hundred yards away. *I better turn that way slower than time.*

The birds and doe ignored him. The birds scattered as they moved closer. He sought the red head of a tom or the beard that would also indicate a male. *Got to have a tom.* Two birds had beards. One stood taller than the rest, but the smaller one was closer and was moving away from the others. *That's a jake. Must be, it's so small. And it's got a small beard. But I don't care. It's a turkey-bird and I'm going home with my first bird. By myself. Come on, bird. Move closer.*

The bird held its head up, scratched once with one foot, twice with the other and looked down to study the ground. It repeated the pattern and walked forward. It was finally far enough away from the others that his shot would not hit another bird. He turned the shotgun slightly, aimed and squeezed the trigger.

The bird dropped. The others flew. The doe ran.

The boy jumped up, stumbled over his leafy camouflage, fell and pulled the trigger again on his semi-automatic weapon as he went down. The shot went into the ground. So did the end of the shotgun barrel.

His breath exploded as he crashed against the ground. He lay still for a few minutes as he tried to breathe again. He felt each rock he landed on as if it were a blast from the shotgun. He stood up, lifted the shotgun and looked at the end of the barrel. Dirt clogged it. He ejected the last shell and put it into a pocket. He pulled the leafy camouflage over his head, packed it into his carry bag and hung the strap over his shoulder. With the shotgun in one hand, he scooted over to his bird.

Holding the bird by both feet, he draped it over his free shoulder and headed back to camp. He almost bounced with excitement all the way back and the walk seemed shorter than when he headed out three hours earlier. But the excitement of the hunt faded when he reached camp and found the two adults still snoring away the afternoon.

He dropped his bird on the camphouse floor and shook his father.

"Pa, wake up. I got myself a tom turkey."

Pa sat up, shook his head as if to shake a cat out of his hair. "What? What did you say? You went out hunting? By yourself?"

"Yeah, Pa. You and Uncle Sammy were dead to the world after all them beers. I went out and got me a turkey."

"Howcome you didn't wake me up? You got no bissness out there in them woods by yerself."

Pa looked down at the bird.

"Good God, Boy. That ain't no tom turkey. You done killed one of them rare bearded hen turkeys."

PISTOL-PACKING MAMA

She saw *Psycho* when she was fourteen and, like the rest of the audience, screamed bloody murder. She refused to take another shower. Even when she lived in a dorm in college, she refused to shower. She managed four years of spit baths instead. She locked her dorm room door and angled a chair beneath the knob every night. Her roommate put up with her fears only three weeks before demanding another room.

Her groom was shocked to learn she slept with a loaded pistol under her pillow. Not just loaded, but with the safety off. When she bathed, the weapon rested on the tub siding. She always bathed facing the open bathroom door.

Three years of marriage was all he could stand, even when she reminded him that Audie Murphy, hero of World War II, slept with a loaded pistol under his pillow.

Her years of caution earned her a variety of nicknames and a lot of behind-the-hands giggles from friends.

The Saturday night of the party for her eightieth birthday finally ended and everyone left. She locked the front door, doubled-checked the back door, locked herself in the bedroom and slid the .38 special, safety off, beneath her pillow.

The dream woke her. She sat up screaming and realized it was not the dream but the bedroom door creaking open. The street light showed a stranger in the doorway. He wore bedraggled clothing and a smirk. The knife in his hand caught the outside light.

"Just you and me, lady. We gonna have some fun."

She reached under the pillow, seized the pistol and pulled it out. "Fun is right. I've waited almost seventy years for you."

She emptied the pistol and called 911.

Nobody laughed at her again.

THE POACHING BROTHERS

Gerald knew the Wilkinson boys hunted over bait. But catching them was already a two-year project. This morning, opening day, the Widow Miss Bertha had reinforced his opinion with her phone call.

"I found where they gutted a deer on my side of the fence," she had said. "The coyotes hadn't gotten to it yet, but the buzzards had. And there was corn scattered all over."

She had invited him to come see for himself. Together they had followed the deer's blood trail back to her landline. Miss Bertha had gone home. "I'm not about to go over there." She pointed across the fence and went home.

Alone, he had walked acre after acre, but no clue. He had found where the deer had been shot, but ever-widening circles led him only to a tall pine and a climbing stand waiting for the next hunt. For more than thirty feet up, the pine was limbless, but stubs showed where someone had hacked off numerous limbs to be able to climb over them. Bark had been sliced that high from the blades of the stand.

But he saw no corn near the stand. No sign of where corn had been dumped near the stand. He followed a trail across the steep-banked creek circling through the property. On the other side, about thirty feet from the crossing, he found another stand hanging at the foot of a sweetgum which had also been trimmed. He scouted the area in ever-widening circles until he knew no corn was in shooting sight.

He removed his cap and wiped sweat from his forehead with his sleeve.

Hot for opening day. He took a deep breath and let it out slowly. In place, he turned, scanned the area he had searched and shook his head, perplexed.

Damn it. I know they've got corn out here somewhere. I'll get back out here tomorrow and wait for them. Ticks and red bugs be damned. I am not gonna let this go on another year.

He headed toward the Wilkinson house but stayed far enough in the woods that unless one of the brothers looked directly toward him he wouldn't be seen. He spotted a large oak flanked with a sweetgum sapling covered with honeysuckle and sawbriar vines.

Perfect place to hide and watch. I'll see you boys tomorrow.

An hour before dawn, Gerald sat in his truck and ate his wife's biscuit stuffed with egg and ham and sipped coffee from his thermos. He leaned over the steering wheel and looked for the moon in the west. It was far enough above setting that he would not need a flashlight. He took the last bite of his breakfast and another swallow of coffee and wiped his mouth with his handkerchief.

Time to go.

He hunkered down against the oak tree before the moon slipped behind the western canopy. The night wind slept. The moonlight glistened frost on the leaves overhead. Gerald opened his thermos and sipped coffee.

Better go slow on this. Don't want to have to hike my leg just as they come out.

Patience was not one of his natural virtues, but he had learned that to catch a poacher he had to have patience. He had learned to sit long hours.

The moon fell below the horizon before the sun highlighted the trees overhead. A pre-dawn breeze stirred. Lights flashed on in one room and then another. Two figures moved through the lights. They entered the kitchen and Gerald heard voices but couldn't make out the words. One of the boys stood at the stove. Gerald watched a few moments through his binoculars and let them dangle around his neck as he realized the brother was cooking breakfast. In spite of his having eaten, when the smell of bacon reached him, his mouth watered and his stomach growled.

Shoulda kept my biscuit till I got here.

Along with the temptation of the bacon, laughter floated to him.

Enjoy yourself while you can, boys. You gonna be in jail tonight.

He took another sip of coffee, replaced the lid and stood up.

Better hike my leg while I can.

He took two steps to his left. A deer snorted, stomped, snorted and fled.

Damnation.

"Sump'n spooked that-air deer," came from the house.

"Probably one of them coyotes. We oughta git ourselves out to them stands right quick like. Them coyotes gonna have the deer running every which-a-way. You bout done with ya bacon biscuits?"

"Yeah. Let's go."

Gerald tended to business, wiped his hands on the seat of his pants and settled back down. He raised his miniature Nikon binoculars and studied the front porch.

The two men walked out, clad in camouflage, each carrying a long barreled firearm. From his view with the binoculars, he thought they both carried .12 gauge shotguns. With double-ought buckshot these were perfect for the forest they hunted.

Which one do I follow? Which one will lead me to the corn?

Jake, the older, headed off to the east, into the rising sun.

Not the one to follow. I'll be sunblind and all he has to do is look back and see me. I'll follow Sammy.

Sammy headed north toward the stand in the pine. His flashlight served as a guide for Gerald who wasn't about to turn on his own light. But after about 100 yards, the light went out. Gerald hunkered down behind brush growing beside a poplar and hoped he would blend in with the limbs and few leaves that had managed to hold on in spite of the cold nights.

A few minutes later, he heard the scraping of a climbing stand moving up the pine.

Just give him time. Let him shoot. I'll have him for sure.

Dawn came. Jays welcomed the day. A pair of geese flew overhead. A cardinal greeted the morning.

Cardinals up. I reckon the turkeys are off the roost. I'd think they'd be around here after the corn. Funny I haven't seen or heard any.

The cold deepened, and Gerald shivered. It would be another hour before the morning began to warm.

Gerald did not have to wait another hour.

A doe came busting from his left, with a forkhorn buck behind her. Neither slowed down as they charged by him and Sammy. Gerald saw Sammy lift the shotgun and then raise the barrel to point up. The deer disappeared off to his right.

Probably decided the buck was too small or going too fast. Good thinking on his part for a change.

A few minutes later tall antlers appeared over the brush. The buck materialized as it ambled toward Sammy from behind his stand. It would be silent in the frost-damp hardwood leaves and unseen until it passed Sammy.

Sammy's gonna shoot this way. He went flat and crawled behind the poplar. Sammy shot. And whooped.

Jake whooped back.

Gerald did not move. He waited for the sound of Sammy's stand to scrape the pine bark as he walked it down. And for Jake to arrive. He'd catch them both.

Jake came running up about the time Sammy reached the ground.

"What'cha get?" He hollered while still some yards away.

"Got that big un we been watching all year. Ten points."

Gerald ambled around the poplar and said, "Hey, fellows. Game warden."

"Hey, come see my deer. He's a big un."

Gerald looked at the buck. Ten points, heavy beams, long tines. A true trophy for this area where the deer had been hunted heavily for several years and few bucks made it to their third year.

"Need to see your licenses, fellas," he said.

Neither man hesitated. Both reached into hip pockets and pulled out wallets with big game licenses and deer tags.

"I see you've used one of your tags each," he said. "You butcher them yourselves or take them somewhere?"

"We kain't afford them butchers. They charge $75 dollars to cut up a deer that don't weight no more'n sixty pounds. We do our'n."

"You boys want to field dress this one out right here? I've heard there's corn out here. Let's take a look at what's in this fella's gut."

"Sure." Sammy said. "My deer had a belly full of corn. Got no idea where about he got it. Let's see iffen this here one is filled up too."

Gerald watched, amazed at how quickly the two worked. In five minutes they had castrated the buck, slit it up the belly and pulled out the insides.

"This here be its stomach," Sammy said as if the ranger had no idea about a deer's insides. "Let's see what he been eating."

Sammy stabbed the stomach and did not flinch at the smell of the escaped gas. Gerald did not let himself flinch either.

"Looks like he got some corn jest like that other one. Where in blue hell he getting corn around here?" Sammy said.

"I'll take a look around," Gerald said. "You go hang your deer and get him hosed down. I'll stop by your house in a little bit."

The brothers dragged the buck toward the house while Gerald considered searching the land again.

Won't do me a bit of good. They've got it hid, but where? Where?

He pondered while he walked toward where that buck had come from. He reached the creek and followed it as it curled into a C. Where had that buck crossed?

He looked back for the stand, lined it up with the poplar where he had hidden, and followed the creek until he was as close as he could figure the buck was when he first saw it. The creek flowed about ten yards to his right.

A deep-cut path led to the creek bank.

Not much of a crossing. Just wide enough for deer. Too steep and too deep for people. Well, maybe not. Just about ten or so feet. Lot deeper here than where I crossed before.

He looked down at his new boots and shrugged. *Oh well, I gotta get 'em wet someday.*

He grabbed a hold on a sapling that grew from the creek bank and tried to ease down the bank, but his boot cleats picked up mud and he skidded the last three feet. He landed with a splash in ankle-deep water.

Three yards downstream, where the creek curved, a doe and yearling leaped from inside the tall bank, snorted and fled downstream.

What the hell?

He considered walking downstream on the mud beside the stream but a glance into the creek bed reminded him it was filled with pebbles. He chose the safer path and splashed a few steps downstream. The bank had been undercut by floods over the years.

Damned if that's not a cave yonder. They did jump out of the creek bank. I wonder—

A trough tucked out of sight from anyone walking alongside held two inches of corn. The area still smelled of the does and the musk from the ten-pointer.

He stuffed a handful of corn into his pocket. *Take the brothers to the jail and the deer to the soup kitchen. A perfect November day.*

He smiled as he scrambled up the bank and headed for the house.

THE BIRD MAN

Driving through Nebraska on his way home from Yellowstone, he noticed a scarecrow standing in what had once been a corn field. Only stubble remained, but crows fed everywhere. He slowed. Two crows perched on the scarecrow. *A scarecrow that didn't scare crows? What's the point?*

What's the point of anything anyhow? You get born. You struggle to live. You get forced to retire and what have you got? Time to kill. And time kills.

The image of the two crows remained with him when he reached home. He'd been gone three weeks and his bird feeders were empty. Before he unloaded his luggage and Yellowstone mementoes, he filled four feeders with mixed bird seed. When he returned from the garage with the meal worms for the bluebird feeder, a dozen birds were already at the other feeders. The scarecrow's image superimposed itself on his feeders.

Wouldn't it be fun to see them perched on a scarecrow?

He smiled and filled the bluebirds' feeder with the mealworms. *Time to unload the car.*

He took everything inside but didn't unpack mementoes or luggage. Instead, he sat at the kitchen table and thought. His feeders were in the front yard for passersby to see the birds and, he hoped, get the idea to put up feeders themselves. None of his close neighbors had taken the hint. But maybe if he built a scarecrow he would get some attention and maybe others would become birders.

The scarecrow can't be like the one in Nebraska. I want the birds to see it as a feeder. It just cannot look ratty. It has to appeal to the neighbors. Something attractive. Maybe something like Rodin's The Thinker, *just add a graduation cap with a rim to keep the feed from falling off and maybe let him hold up a hand with a plate.*

Decision made, he unpacked, stowed everything away and headed to the grocery. He'd tackle construction tomorrow and let his sleep determine the details. *To sleep, to dream, to decide.*

Morning found the first snowfall spattering white across the yard. Birds shivered on the dogwoods' barren limbs. Inside, he sketched his ideas.

Undeterred by the snow, he headed to Home Depot for material which he unloaded in the driveway as the snow tapered off. He dragged out the Black and Decker work bench and skill saw. He framed a body, a bench for it to sit on, 2X4's for legs, a 4x4 for an arm that rested on the knee. He hunted up an old plastic pumpkin for the head. He set the dummy on a glider that dated back almost sixty years, to his days sliding under his first car to change the oil. He searched his closet for discards and found a pair of too small cargo pants and a long-sleeve shirt that was worn thin but not ready for the rag bag. The clothing shouldn't annoy the neighbors. He studied the pumpkin head and discarded it. He made a block head for the figure and covered it with a piece of the camouflage he had used when he went duck hunting. He topped it with a rimmed, flat board that was to serve as the feeder. He added another rimmed board to the outstretched arm.

He rolled it into the front yard and the birds scattered at the sight. He poured sunflower seeds and mixed grains on the two platforms and went inside to see if the birds would venture to the new feeding platforms.

Not that day. A few came to the feeders they knew. Two squirrels found the feed and by afternoon had cleaned both platforms.

Early the next morning, he refilled both.

That afternoon, a wren ventured to the "hat" platform. Another followed. Although squirrels competed with the birds, the birds continued to feed.

And best of all, on the fourth day as he watched out the front window, a neighbor drove by, stopped and backed up to look.

For a week, Jennie Johnston stopped and watched the birds every day. On the eighth day, Jennie came to his door with a suggestion. "Why don't you dress up like your dummy and see if they'll eat out of your hand?"

"Ok, I never thought of that. I will!"

How the heck can I make a hat from a board? Or a feeder that I can hold for hours? I can't use a wooden tray. I'll just go to Target and buy a tea tray and fix it to sit on my knee. That way I can balance it without having to hold it up all the time.

At Target he purchased two aluminum trays.

He hunted up his high school football helmet, removed the padding, drilled three holes and bolted a tray to the helmet. *An aluminum tray—a lot lighter than trying to hold a board on this tired old neck. And I need another set of scarecrow clothes.*

He rooted into his few remaining yard-work clothes and dressed for the adventure, once again wearing his football helmet. He rolled the office chair from his desk into the yard. If he were going to be the dummy he wanted a back rest. No way he could sit for hours without one. He placed it beside the dummy-scarecrow and towed the dummy back into the garage.

He returned with a small bucket of bird feed. He sat and dipped a handful of bird feed on the top-hat tray and some on his tea tray. He had to sit still. *I wonder how long I can sit here as arthritic as my back and joints are?*

The birds that fled when he came out with the chair had taken refuge in the dogwoods scattered along the west side of his yard. In minutes, they returned to feast on the human-dummy's food supply. As squirrels crossed the yard and climbed onto his knee, he jounced his knee slightly and the squirrels realized he was real. They fled. The birds, however, seemed to consider any movement as natural as a limb shifting in the wind. Some perched on the tray on his head, some on the tray he held on his knee.

He longed to reach out to touch the feathers, to feel the softness, but dared not. Cardinals, flickers, Carolina wrens, a jay, an oriole, bluebirds, all saw him only as another dummy who supplied food. Life was no longer something he longed to escape but had become something to love and to live.

As Jennie drove up, she stopped and waved. He lifted his left hand and the birds flew. Jennie called, "Sorry. I didn't mean to scare the birds."

He smiled and waved again. "They'll get used to us waving."

She nodded, waved again and drove on. From that day on, she slowed and lifted her hand as she drove by. He always lifted his left hand in reply. In a week, the birds no longer fled when he responded to Jennie.

Some days he sat outside with the birds for hours. Cold did not keep him inside, but rain did. He would then pull out the dummy and sit by the picture window and watch.

Day seventeen, snow returned. Large soft flakes tried to stay airborne. He pulled his office chair into the yard, donned the helmet, carried out the bucket of feed and settled down with the feed beside him. He filled his trays and enjoyed the snow and the birds as they flitted from the dogwoods to his servers and back.

Three hours later, Jennie drove up, slowed and waved. He did not wave back. She stopped, cut the motor and called. "Mr. Simmons? You all right?" No reply. She approached him, touched his shoulder and the body fell into the snow.

THE TELEVISION SET

She was tired after forty years of tending to the five-thousand-acre ranch. Now all the cattle and horses were sold and she could prop her feet up and enjoy not riding the range or mucking stalls or pushing cattle to the sale barn.

The hunters who now leased the land paid more than enough to cover her real estate tax and to support her everyday needs, with some left over for savings.

Today, some of that wildlife money was going to pay for a new large-screen TV. Delivery day for her was as important as delivery day for parents—her new baby was arriving.

Into the den came first the large wooden cabinet, five feet long, with sliding doors in front for her to see everything connected: The cable box, her new DVD/tape player and CD player. Retirement years were now going to be filled with adventures and trips to national parks, safaris in Africa and visits to crime labs. Forget those mystery novels that hinted at the details or the shady romance novels. She would enjoy *real* life.

The two men spent the morning working and hauling. By noon, everything was in place and they showed her how to use the remote to control everything.

She said, "The color is fabulous. But I thought I was getting a Samsung. What is this TV company? R-L-TV?"

"I think it's a new company. It's *Real Life Television.* And it's 4-D. I'm sorry, but that's the one that had your name on it. Do you want us to take it back? It's guaranteed anyhow, for six months. You can return it for any reason for that long. It's the only 4-D that has that kind of guarantee. "

"Oh, no, I don't want to wait another day. It looks fine to me."

They left. She settled down to watch. First, Fox news, then CNN, and thought, *I don't need to waste my time on that bickering.*

She went to History, but they were showing Hitler and people trying to find out if he actually had committed suicide or gone to South America. On she searched. Animal Planet was visiting the Kalahari Desert and she found two meerkat families faced off in a battle for territory. She leaned back in her recliner and watched Flower and her band win the battle and then teach the youngsters to forage for food.

The camera angle changed and showed a stray male searching for a female to run off with him. He galloped toward the camera and leaped from the TV screen into her den.

She shrieked and stood up. The meerkat froze on the carpet, looked at her, turned, leaped back into the Kalahari and ran from the camera.

"That didn't happen," she said. "I can't believe that happened. No, it didn't happen. I just wished for one of those darlings to be here. It didn't happen."

The meerkats continued to forage and as their day ended, they returned to their burrow and the program ended.

She fixed supper, put her soup and sandwich on a tray and returned to the den to watch and eat.

Watch what? Maybe another wildlife show. She clicked the remote to view each channel to see the programs underway. "Ah, a deer." She selected that channel, dropped the remote onto the sofa, but missed and it fell unnoticed onto the floor. She began to eat while watching.

Hunters sat in a blind. *Oh, I don't want to see them kill a deer.* But as she reached for the remote that was not on the sofa, she saw several deer move through the woods in front of the blind. Three does and two fawns whose spots were barely visible went to the same spot, dropped their heads and seemed to be eating. *What are they eating? Have the hunters put out food? I reckon they aren't going to kill the deer. They put out food to take pictures.*

Someone shot. The five deer panicked. One of the fawns ran toward the camera and landed in her den.

She leaped up, spilling soup and sandwich onto the floor.

The fawn dashed across the room, ran around the sofa, headed back toward the TV and reappeared in the woods as it continued to run away.

She gasped. "No, that did not happen. I just got scared. This 4-D TV is just plain scary."

She turned off the TV and cleaned up the floor.

"I think I'll run up to the DQ and eat a hamburger and have one of their shakes. Take a book. I gotta get used to this 4-D stuff."

The Dairy Queen was thirty miles away, twenty of them on a rough dirt road. Almost two hours later, she was back to watch. She went to a news channel and listened to the moderators attack the president.

I can't watch that. I'll find another animal program.

She searched the guide and discovered a program about the rise of the black wolf in Yellowstone. She settled down to watch the black pup go from a pack member to a lone wolf. He cornered an elk in a creek and leaped for the kill. He missed. And landed in her den.

She screamed. The wolf looked at her, bared his teeth. His hackles rose. She waved her arms. The predator turned and leaped away. And landed in the snow in Yellowstone.

That did not happen. I must be going crazy. There is no way anything is coming out of the TV into my house.

She turned it off and headed for her *medicine* cabinet—a glass of medicinal scotch on the rocks would solve this illusion and she would sleep the night through.

Morning came, and with it the newspaper. She checked the news. Nothing but the usual attacks on the president. She had her second coffee while she enjoyed her puzzles. Sudoku was tough, but the numbers fell into place. Her literary mind was quick with words and she finished the crossword easily. She was ready for more TV.

The Big Cat Diary was on. Mama Cat had left her cubs to hunt, and the camera stayed on the two cubs while the narrator told of their danger with nearby hyenas trying to sniff out the babies. One of the cubs began to ease from its hidey-hole, toward the camera. A hyena yipped. The cub leaped.

And landed in her den.

Its only movement was shivering. Afraid.

"It's not there," she told herself. "It'll disappear in a second. Just like everything else has."

The cub did not move. On the screen, the mother lion returned and chased off the hyenas. She lay down to feed her cubs, but only one came to her nipples.

The cub in the den sat and stared at the lady, who stared back.

Maybe it is real, she thought. She held down a hand and wiggled her fingers.

The cub came to her and sniffed her fingers. She reached down, picked it up and snuggled it to her chest. "You don't weigh anything, but you are real," she said. "But what in the hell can I do with you? Put you in a zoo? Maybe if I throw you back, you can go back."

She gritted her teeth, closed her eyes and tossed the cub toward the TV.

She heard the *thunk* and opened her eyes. The cub rolled on the floor. A commercial ran on the TV.

"Oh my goodness, little one. Are you hurt?"

She ran over and lifted the cub. It snuggled to her.

She set it on the sofa beside her and searched her smart phone for the federal wildlife officials. When she finally reached someone, she said, "I have just gotten a lion cub, and I need to get information on what to do with it." She was told it was illegal to have a lion cub and who was she and where was she?

She hung up. No way she was going to jail because of the funny TV.

"Little one, what the hell can I do with you?"

The commercial ended. The cub ran to the TV and leaped.

The next morning, she answered a knock on her door. Two federal officials stood on her porch. "We came to get the lion cub," one said.

"What lion cub?" she asked.

"The one you called about yesterday."

"Oh, that. I don't have it any more. I tried to throw it back to Africa, but couldn't. It jumped back instead when the commercial was over."

She closed the door and returned to her TV to watch *Mountain Men*. Eustace was cutting trees to make money to pay bills and maybe have enough to buy more land. He felled one tree that didn't fall but hung up in one he was not supposed to cut. She shook her head—she had once had the same problem. When he tackled the next tree, she said, "That cameraman better back off. That tree is gonna fall on him."

It missed the cameraman but fell from the TV into her den, across the sofa, and a limb pierced her chest.

The commercial came on and she sat up. *How come my chest hurts?*

THE HIKER AND PHOTOGRAPHER

"Run," **he shouted** as he fled down the trail toward her. Behind him charged a bull moose, its head lowered, antlers leading. He grunted with every leap.

"Don't run," she yelled back. "He'll chase you."

He paid no heed but kept running. She jumped behind a tree.

The moose passed her and continued after the man. She watched in horror as it reached the hiker and gored him. Blood colored the world.

She screamed and woke herself.

It was the TV program I watched at the hotel last night. About the woman walking her dog somewhere and being found dead. Where was it? Doesn't really matter where. Just somewhere. The husband was arrested for murder, found guilty and sent to jail. Two years later, some investigator figured out the woman had been gored to death by a bull moose and the husband was turned loose.

No wonder I had a nightmare, seeing those four bull elk on my way to this campground. Lots bigger than the mule deer I saw last year. And bigger than that dream moose. Maybe I shouldn't be camping out here by myself. I don't know anybody else out here. If I got stomped to death by an elk or clawed to death by a bear, who would miss me for the next two weeks? Nobody even knows where I am.

School out and lesson plans finished for next September, she was on her own for these last two weeks of freedom before returning to the uneducated hoards who considered themselves geniuses because they had made it to college and now knew all there was to know. Just sit out the four years for the degree that would prove to the world they were indeed geniuses.

Escape to the mountains was her answer. Escape the lesson plans and the idea of returning to the classroom. At least here she could relax if she could only get school out of her mind. The nightmare, bad as it was, did just that.

She turned over, closed her eyes, wiggled against the air mattress for comfort and tried to return to sleep.

No good. Something moved outside. Someone passing her tent and headed for the bathroom from the sound of his shuffling. She smelled something. Not a skunk. Not stinky enough to pierce the odor down to her lungs but stinky enough. It wasn't someone going to the bathroom. It was outside her tent. It snuffled. It climbed onto the table where she had left her cooking pot and Coleman stove. Something crashed to the ground. *The stove. It's a bear. He's thrown the stove off the table. God help me if he decides I'm going to be his supper.*

She felt around inside the tent. Somewhere in the pocket under the window was the whistle the ranger told her to blow off and on when she hiked. She had taken it out of her cargo pants pocket and dropped it into the small pocket of the tent. Finally, her fingers felt the cool plastic. She stuck it into her mouth and blew as loud as she could.

The bear ran. And carried the heavy smell with him. *At least most of his stink.*

Somebody called nearby. "What's the matter? Do you need help?"

Other voices called, "What's the matter?"

She yelled, "It was a bear. I whistled to scare him off. I'm okay. Thank you."

The campground quieted down. She tried to go back to sleep, but her mind kept jumping from one idea to another.

We are not the top of the food chain.

We are not the only predators in the mountains.

We may eat some of the wildlife but some of them eat us.

She feared returning to the dream about the moose. She turned onto her other side. An hour later, still awake, she heard the rain begin and the wind rise.

I reckon I'll have a late breakfast. The rain turned her mind back to the days she heard it rattle on the tin roof of the three-room farmhouse where she was reared. She slept.

The rain had ended when she awoke to the smell of coffee and the sound of voices. She slipped on yesterday's pair of cargoes and a button-up long-sleeve cotton shirt and stuck her feet, without socks, into her hiking boots. She unzipped her tent and looked out at the morning. Sunlight streamed through the trees. Even the air glowed green.

Beautiful day. Still smells like last night's rain.

She crawled out of the tent and stood up. A camper who had arrived after she had zipped herself into her own tent greeted her from the adjacent site. "You the one who whistled that bear away last night?"

"Yeah," she replied. She shivered as she remembered. "It scared the willies out of me. I'd just dreamed about somebody getting killed by a moose." She looked at him and thought *why does he look familiar* but couldn't figure why.

Her Coleman stove was right where she had left it last night. It must have been his stove the bear got a hold of.

"Well, the bear's long gone and there're no moose around here that I know of."

She laughed. "I'm Barbra. But I did see elk when I drove in late yesterday." She walked the few feet toward him and extended her hand.

"I'm Fred. You like some coffee?"

"I would, but I hate to take yours. I've got plenty and can fix some."

"Oh, help yourself. Here." He picked up a cup, poured coffee and extended it to her. "Cream or sugar? I've got Coffemate."

"Oh, this is fine. Thanks."

"Pull up a corner," he invited her as he sat on the bench on one side of his table. He pointed to the other side.

She sat. "You just here overnight?"

"No, I'll be here a few days. I'm a photographer and plan to shoot whatever wildlife I can find. Might run up on your bear." He smiled.

"You can have him. I hope I don't run up on him again. Last night, just hearing him and smelling him was enough."

"You missed the skunk and the fox. They came by right after first light. Too dark to get the fox, but I did catch the skunk."

"Skunks and foxes I can live with," she said. "You look familiar. Have we met and I can't remember where or when?"

"I don't think so. I hate to think I'd be easy to forget." He smiled.

"Maybe it's you just look a little like someone I know. I'll figure it out. Don't pay me any mind. I'm a teacher and see probably more than a hundred students every year. You must just look like one of them. That's all."

She finished her coffee, thanked him and wished him luck on his camera hunt.

She gathered her bathing supplies and headed for the shower. When she came back, dressed and ready for her hike, Fred had packed up his food and cooking items and gone in search of critters.

The day was moving along and she thought of John Wayne's words in one of his movies. *Now I'm the one burning daylight and I don't even have to saddle up my horse or drive cattle.*

She made a ham sandwich and ate it while she loaded a belly pack with energy bars and two water bottles. She stowed her cooler on the back seat of her SUV and pulled her cane out. She loved using it. Hand-made by a ranger friend for his own use several years ago and given to her by his widow. The ranger had helped her several times with poachers on her family farm and the two families had become friends. She thought of Bob every time she hiked.

She hung the whistle around her neck, strapped on her belly pack and headed to the trailhead on the north side of the campground. Her map showed it to be steep, but it led to a waterfall. Her point-and-shoot camera would collect it as a remembrance of the trail.

The trail twisted and turned. *Like the streets of Boston. Like they cut the trail when they followed a pig—oh, my, no. They must have followed that bull snake or its cousin through the woods.* She stopped to watch it slither away into the brush. "Okay, fellow, don't feast on any birds. Somebody'll call you a predator and chop your head off. You're close to the bottom of the food chain."

Another mile up the trail, she spotted Fred hunched down, camera in hand. He turned as she neared. He lifted his left hand, finger extended to his mouth to signal silence. She stopped. He turned back to his camera and moved slightly.

She wanted to ease up to see what he was shooting, but respected his need for silence. She remained still. Any wildlife in front of him would flee if she approached.

He rose, moved a few feet off the trail.

Some large animal crashed toward them through the brush.

"Run," Fred yelled.

"No, Fred, don't run. Hide. Behind a tree." But she knew he would not.

She hid behind a large oak a few feet off the trail.

Fred ran down toward her. Behind him charged a bull elk, his ten-by-ten rack lowered. It caught Fred twenty feet from her and tossed him into the air. Fred landed, the bull elk lowered his head and gored the dying body.

She screamed. The elk froze a moment and looked her way. She tried to melt into the tree. The elk bugled, turned and ran into the brush.

THE MOONSHINER AND THE REVENUERS

Mookie Stevens smiled. He had outfoxed the federal revenuer Mr. Jackson for more'n two years. He carried two five-gallon buckets out the kitchen door onto the porch and let the screen slap to behind himself. Down the steps, he headed for the dog pen. If Jackson were watching, he'd see Mookie tending to the dogs. Jackson didn't know he fed the dogs before daylight.

The buckets carried corn and sugar.

The dogs barked and yipped in their hogwire pen as he neared. He unhooked the plywood door and entered. "You sit yo'self." Mookie's voice floated from the pen, across the yard and down the hollow. The barking stopped as the black-and-tan male and the redbone bitch sat.

Mookie crossed the pen and descended ten feet down rough-hewn stairs into the gulley. While the dogs watched, he set the buckets down, unfastened six hooks, removed a three-foot-wide panel, brought the buckets through and fastened another six hooks on the outside.

He stood in a twenty-foot deep gulley extending from inside his dog pen more than two hundred yards to the creek.

Ole Mista Jackson might know where-ats my still, but he ain't never knowed when I be there.

Since he didn't distill in daylight, smoke did not betray him. He never walked down to the creek with a lantern but got there in daylight and napped before he cooked. Nobody knew when he was there.

This July day, with the sun bearing down, the creek tinkling nearby, and sweat coursing down his back, he was mixing mash when he heard footsteps coming down his hidden pathway.

"Hey, Mookie, you here?" His Uncle Jesse.

What's he doing here? Sure he knows the federals watch out for me being here.

Mookie shoved his stirring stick down into the barrel and hustled toward his uncle.

"Hey. There you are. Yer mama axed me to fetch you. She—"

Mookie waved his hands at his uncle. Too late.

Two white faces appeared over the banks.

"Yes indeed, there you are, Mookie Stevens. Gotcha!" Agent Jackson said.

The men stood, each holding a .12 gauge shotgun. Mookie knew both weapons would be loaded with double ought buckshot.

Jimmy, a white boy Mookie knew from childhood and now a Georgia State investigator, stood beside Jackson.

"Oh gawd, Mookie," the uncle said. "I dun give ya away."

Mookie watched the men scamper down the bank. There was nowhere to run. The path would only take him home and they would catch him there. He shoved his hands into his overalls pockets and waited for his trip to the local jail.

The federal agent handcuffed Mookie. "Took me two years to get you, Mookie. But now you'll be getting jail time. I hope a lot of jail time. And you, nigger," he pointed to Mookie's uncle, "you get outta here lessen you want to go to jail too. Tell his ma he won't be coming." He smiled. "And thank you for letting us know Mookie was working. He's been hard to catch down in this hole."

Mookie watched Uncle Jesse skedaddle back toward the dog pen. *Ma'll jest be wanting money, like always. I ain't gonna be having none to give her now. Uncle Jesse wouldn't even have ten dollars in his pocket for her or to help pay my fine or feed my kids while I'm on the chain gang.*

"You take him in, Jack," Jimmy said. "You've worked hard to catch him, and I just happened along today. I'll bust this all up. No need for both of us to get all nasty. I'll plug everything," he raised the shotgun, "and use Mookie's own ax to chop it all up too." He nodded toward the ax propped against the pile of wood.

"Hey, thanks," Jackson said. He pushed Mookie toward the bank. "Up you go, nigger. Off to the jail."

They topped the bank, entered the woods and followed the path the lawmen had worn out from a dirt road almost a mile away. Less than a hundred yards down the trail Mookie heard the shotgun—Jimmy shooting holes in his barrels. Buckshot holes were bad enough, but an ax would for sure make everything worthless. He'd have a hard time replacing the barrels and especially the tubing. *Too bad Jimmy wasn't in with the sheriff or he'd not bust it all up.*

Everybody says my shine the best. Be a long time now afore they get the best again.

Mookie sat in his cell at the jail for almost two hours and was surprised when the sheriff told him he could go if he promised to be in court in Macon come Monday. "You got to be there at ten o'clock in the morning. Any later or you don't show up, you'll be in a heap of trouble. You don't mess with the federals. You understand?"

He promised. The sheriff gave him a paper and told him to take it to Macon with him and give it to the officer in the courtroom.

Mookie couldn't read but he folded it and eased it into his overall's breast pocket.

"You got a long walk home, boy," the sheriff said.

"Nawsuh, hit's not that fur. I'll be home afore the moon gits down."

At home, Mookie fretted and could not bring himself to go down to the remains of his still. He'd have to find another location anyhow, and somehow find a way to rebuild.

He figured he might ought to wear something fancy to the court, but he had nothing fancy, just his farm overalls. He would at least wear a clean pair and a shirt underneath the straps. And take every dollar he had so he could maybe stay out of jail.

Annie cried when he told her he had to go to Macon and if he didn't have enough money he might not be home.

"What I gonna do to feed the chullun?" Twelve black faces looked up to their father.

"You goan come home, Pa?"

"I be home. I tell de judge I gotta be home to feed you. Don't you fret none."

He worried all the way to Macon. If he'd been caught by the sheriff back home, all he had to do was share his makings. But not with the federals.

He had to ask how to find the federal courthouse when he got to Macon. At the door, he showed his paper to a man in uniform and was directed to the courtroom. There, another uniformed man took his paper and told him to sit until his name was called. Mookie watched the officer take the paper up to the front and hand it to a tall skinny white man wearing a black suit and almost no hair. They talked a minute and then the officer pointed to Mookie.

Time passed so slow he thought a snapping turtle could have walked to Macon from his still. People moved around the room. Fans overhead whumped the smell of sweat and stale tobacco around. Mookie gnawed a finger raw while he waited. When it began to bleed, he pressed the spot on his overall leg.

A door up front opened and an officer yelled, "All rise!"

The judge strode in, stepped up to his seat and sat.

The officer allowed them all to sit back down.

Mookie's name was called, and he looked down at the finger. Still bleeding. He shoved his hand into his pocket.

He stood, his belly in a knot, wondered what to do.

"You Mookie Stevens?" the tall man asked who stood in front of the judge.

Mookie nodded.

"Well, come on up here." He waved and pointed to a spot on his left.

As Mookie reached the front of the bench, Jimmy, in uniform, walked up and stood on the other side of the man.

"Where's your lawyer?"

"I ain't got no lawyer."

The white man shrugged, turned to the judge and said, "He was caught at a still, stirring up mash. The officers have been after him for about a year."

The judge turned to Jimmy. "You the arresting officer?"

"Yes sir. One of them. Agent Jackson was the federal officer, but he had to be out of town today and asked me to be here."

The judge shuffled papers and looked at Mookie. "What you got to say for yourself, Mookie?"

Mookie continued to look at the front of the bench and not at the judge. "I was making likker, suh. I gotta do something to feed my chullun. I ain't got no regular work. Jest making likker and my garden. And sum-time I gits some farm work."

"How many children you got, Mookie?"

"I gots twelve, Mr. Judge, suh. Please, suh, don't send me to no chain gang. I gotta feed my chullun."

The judge leaned back, studied Mookie, looked at the prosecutor, turned to Jimmy and said "You got anything you want to say?"

"He does have a big family, Your Honor. I think he's scared enough a fine should do."

"You got any money to pay your fine?"

"Yessuh."

"How much you got in your pocket?"

"I brung all I has, suh. Fo-hundred and ten dollars."

The judge leaned forward and stared at Mookie. Mookie had not looked him in the eye. The judge said, "No jail time. Fine is four hundred dollars." He banged his gavel. "Next case."

"What I do, Mr. Judge?"

"Go over there to that lady and give her the money, and then you go home and don't you go making any more liquor and show up here again or you will go to the chain gang. You hear?"

"Yessuh."

Mookie paid his fine and walked out of the building. As he reached his truck, Jimmy and his GBI partner approached.

"Mookie, wait up, you hear?"

He waited. The two men formed a V in front of him. No one would be able to hear or see what happened.

"You been down to your still?" Jimmy asked.

Mookie shook his head. Jimmy smiled. "I emptied that shotgun into a stump. It's all just like you left it. This'll get you back in business right away."

Each passed him two hundred dollars.

Mookie looked at the money and then directly into Jimmy's eyes and smiled.

Jimmy clapped his hand on Mookie's shoulder. "Let us know when the next batch is ready for us to pick up."

THE INHERITANCE

Twelve couples watched her when she walked in. She was alone and a stranger. The Brick was traditionally a couples only restaurant.

Clad in a bright blue pants suit, with a briefcase in hand, she looked over the diners, strolled to one of the three empty tables, turned to look over the diners again and selected her chair.

A waiter hustled over to her. "Ma'am, we usually entertain only couples."

"You can't run me out, Sonny," she said. He smiled, but his face reddened to match his thinning hair. She was younger than he. "I'm an attorney, so you don't want to discriminate. Please bring me a menu."

"Yes, Ma'am."

While he went for the menu, she stood her briefcase in an empty chair and rummaged into it. Out came a spiral-bound notepad and mechanical pencil.

Her gaze locked on that of a man two tables away. She smiled. He frowned. His wife turned to look at the stranger who held her husband's attention.

The lawyer nodded to her and smiled, then wrote something in her notebook.

She flipped the notebook closed as the waiter returned with the menu and a glass of ice water with a wedge of lemon twisted onto the rim and a straw stuck into the glass, paper still hanging over the upper end.

She muttered, "Thanks," to the waiter. He nodded and left. She turned her attention back to her notepad but glanced frequently at the couple.

The waiter returned, and again she flipped the notebook closed. "Are you ready to order?" She had not looked at the menu.

"Oh, just a bowl of French onion soup, thank you. Oh, yes, one more thing. Is that the Morgan Thompsons over at the corner table by the window?"

The waiter nodded, "Yes, Ma'am. Our mayor," and left.

She propped her elbow on the table and her chin on her palm and stared at the man. Her free hand jerked and she nodded as if something had just occurred to her. She opened the notepad and bent over it. The man rose, slapped his napkin onto the table and stalked toward her.

She flipped the cover closed seconds before he hovered over her.

"What are you doing?" he demanded. "You keep staring at me. My wife and I don't like your behavior. You don't even belong in here."

She looked up and smiled. In the sweetest, softest voice she could muster, she replied, "Oh, I think I do belong here. The question now is, do you?"

"What the hell are you writing about me and my wife?" He reached for her notepad.

She jerked it away, held it under the table by her leg. "Uh-uh, my fine friend. It's for you to wonder and me to know. Now be a gentleman and return to your table. Or I'll have to ask the waiter to remove you from here for disturbing me."

"How dare you!" His fists planted on hips, he continued to stare at her.

"Go along, Sonny. Go eat your steak before it gets cold and they have to re-heat it to well done when I know you like it rare."

Her soup arrived. She asked the waiter, "Would you please ask this gentleman to remove himself from my table?"

"Mr. Thompson, sir, I have to ask you to return to your table," the waiter whispered.

Thompson huffed, spun around and stalked to his table.

The next evening, she returned to the same restaurant, stood in the doorway and studied the diners. This time, she held the notepad in her hand. The maître d' approached her, "Would you follow me?" he asked.

"No, thanks. I want the table in the corner down by the windows."

"I'm sorry, but Mr. Thompson usually sits there."

"I don't see anybody at the table now," she replied. "Is this a closed club or something?"

"Well, no, but he usually sits…"

"Tonight, I will sit here," she said and left him standing with menu in hand. She took the seat that put her back to the wall and gave her an open view of the room.

The maitre d' followed, dropped the menu on the table and walked off, shaking his head and muttering to himself.

She placed her pad on the table top and studied the menu. Before the waiter arrived with her water, the Thompson couple entered the restaurant. The mayor stormed toward her.

She looked up and smiled. "Oh, it's you again. I hope you have a good evening."

"That's my table," he growled.

"Oh, I don't see your name on it. Why don't you just sit there?" She pointed to a nearby table.

"Lady, I don't know who you are, but you are...."

His wife touched his arm. "It's all right, Morgan. Let's just sit here." She moved to the next table and sat with her back to the stranger.

He mumbled something the lawyer didn't hear and walked around the table to sit facing both women.

The stranger nodded to herself, opened the notepad and began to write. Every few minutes she looked up at Thompson and nodded as if to herself. Her pencil moved on.

Several other couples had noticed the dispute. And watched.

Water arrived for the Thompsons, but he stood, muttered about the company and held out his hand to his wife. They hustled out.

She smiled and laid her pencil down.

Half-way through her French onion soup she looked up as a woman entered the restaurant, glanced around and strode to her table. She too carried a notepad.

"Hi," she said. "I'm Abigail Morris from the local paper. I was told to come see you for an interview."

The next afternoon, the interview ran in the four-page paper, the headline: "Attorney seeks Thompson heir to multi-million dollar fortune."

"Must be the youngest generation in a direct line from William Tecumseh Morgan Thompson," the story began.

The attorney returned to the restaurant as twilight fell. She again went to the table in the corner.

She had just settled down and opened her notepad when the mayor strode in, alone, and stomped to her table.

"You're looking for me, Miss. I'm Morgan Thompson, great grandson of William Tecumseh Morgan Thompson." He sat.

"You are the youngest Thompson in the line?"

"No, I have a son. He's in college. He's a minor so I speak for him."

"How old—he's under sixteen and in college?"

"Of course he's not sixteen. He's twenty, still a minor by the law."

She stared at him. "You prove it to me. Bring me all the needed papers—birth certificates as far back as they go and any and all other documents you can gather. We don't give out money unless we have the evidence. Now let me enjoy my meal without your sitting there."

"You'll see." He rose and his every step shivered the floor as he stormed out.

From her room in the hotel that night, she called home. "How's the search going?" her husband asked.

"Oh, I don't think I'll have to search. The mayor is all over himself, thinking his son is going to inherit millions. The mayor is not the most beloved citizen. Don't have any idea how he keeps his job unless he's good at stuffing the ballot box. Somebody'll give me the information I need. I'm sure I'll be home before the week's out, with the youngster in tow."

She made no effort to close her notepad when her usual waiter came to her table. He glanced at it, raised his eyebrows and said, "Ma'am, we have the French onion soup you seem to like, but I would suggest you go next door to the diner. They have something—actually some*one*—you would enjoy more."

He winked and repeated, "Some*one*."

"Finally." The word came with a smile that lit her eyes. She placed a fifty dollar bill under her water glass. "I will do just that." She stood.

"You seem to be the first true and honest gentleman I've met here. You have a good evening. A very good evening."

"Thank you, Ma'am. And I must say you are the best portrait artist this town has ever seen. You surely did capture a perfect likeness of our mayor."

Her smile became a mischievous grin as she strode toward the door.

The diner looked like an abandoned streamlined bus, gleaming chrome with aluminum siding faded to a blue-white. Inside, however, the dining area gleamed from scrubbing. Only one other customer, a small girl sitting alone in a booth near the back.

"May I join you?" the lawyer asked.

The child looked up from her coloring book at the visitor, shrugged and nodded. "Okay. Who are you?"

"I'm Sally Middleton, I'm from out of town. And you are?"

The child replied. "I'm Morgan."

The waitress came from behind the counter and placed a glass of ice water on the table. "I see you've met Morgan. This is your first time in here. I make a terrific hamburger and fries."

"I have and she's a charmer. And the menu sounds perfect. By the way, howcome a girl has the name Morgan? Are you a fan of the Earp brothers?"

The waitress smiled. "No, she's not named for Morgan Earp. For her father."

"Is he working late this evening?" She glanced around the room.

The waitress shook her head. "Have no idea. Come on over to the counter while we talk and I grill your supper."

As they walked to the counter, the waitress continued. "Her father and I had a one night stand, which left me pregnant. He took off for college out of state and I haven't seen him since. So, Morgan and I make do together. Tough at times, but I love her so much it's not that tough." She smiled. "Rare or well done?"

"Rare. So what's her father's name, his full name? Morgan who, or who Morgan?"

"Morgan Thompson, named for his father the mayor, which makes our mayor my Morgan's grandpa. Enough said?"

Sally smiled. "Quite enough."

She pulled out a business card. "Can you get me a copy of her birth certificate?"

"Whatever for?"

"You didn't see the paper?"

"The newspaper? No."

"You know the red-headed waiter at the Brick?"

"Yeah. He's my brother."

"Well, he read the paper and knew why I'm in town. And referred me here. I'm looking for the youngest generation of the Thompson family. You apparently are not it, but you are the mother of it. Your daughter inherits a few million in cash and securities plus about five thousand acres of that wild land just down the road."

KITTY KAT

I don't know how long I lay there on my belly, with my head twisted sideways, but when I opened my eyes all I saw was the narrow-board oak floor leading to the sofa. A patch of sunlight glinted white on the lacquer only inches from my face.

How come I'm on the floor? *I ought to get up.*

My right arm was bent under me, and I pushed up on it and crawled toward the sofa. I remembered getting rapped upside my head and wondered why I wasn't dizzy. *May not be woozy but I'm not gonna take a chance on falling again.* The sofa was a handy pick-me-up. I got onto my knees, placed my fists on the sofa seat and pushed up against the rough corduroy fabric.

Strange. The sofa was a cheapie, and the cushions always kept a dent where I sat or laid my purse or a book. But it hadn't held the imprint of my knuckles where I pushed up. *Oh, well, maybe I used a firmer spot.*

I looked over the sofa and through the picture window. Outside the world hadn't changed. Except my car wasn't in the driveway. My BMW, the car my father gave me when I graduated college with a perfect 4.0 average. A degree that I traded in for the useless M. R. S. that has nearly killed me.

That's how come I got knocked on the head. Somebody came in the house. A man.

I closed my eyes and tried to remember, to pull up his face. Did I see him? Yes. He had no mask. I knew him.

Oh gawd, yes. My ex-husband. He promised to kill me when I left. After I had his butt arrested for hitting me over and over. Not today, though. My head doesn't even hurt where he whomped me. He just hit me and took my car. He couldn't stand it that I drove a fine car and all he had was an old used-up Ford pickup that was rusted long before we got married. That truck should of been enough to warn me off. I reckon I'm just what he used to call a Monday morning quarterback.

Well, I'll show him. I'll call the cops and he'll be back in jail. Unless he took all the money in my purse. That fifteen hundred cash'll get him a long ways. I better call the cops right now. Where'd I leave my purse with my cell phone inside?

I scooted to the kitchen. It should be on the counter by the refrigerator. So should my cane, which I have to use on my walks in the garden. *Uh-uh. No purse. He must have taken it too. And the cell phone. How in heck can I call the cops with no phone? I'll go next door.*

I picked up the cane and reached for the door knob to go to the back yard. My hand just passed over it and the knob appeared through my hand. Impossible. *I must be dreaming. I must not have been hit on the head or anything. I'm in the middle of a nightmare.*

I reached up, ran my hand over my head, but didn't feel anything. Nothing. I felt nothing. Not even my head. But I could feel the cane in my other hand.

I for sure am asleep. Dreaming. Okay. I'll go back in the living room and lie down on the sofa.

Yikes! There I am. Lying on the floor. Right in front of the sofa.
Am I dead?

Blood pooled around my head on the floor. It wasn't wet-red but drying brown.

I must be dead.

I reached down to touch myself. I felt nothing beneath my hand. Then my hand disappeared inside myself.

I screamed. Only I didn't hear my own scream. Still clutching the cane, I ran into the hall.

Kitty Kat sat on the hall table and filled the air with purrs as loud as the whisper of waves on the beach. I reached over to pet her. "Oh, Kitty Kat, what is the matter with me?"

I didn't hear my own words.

But Kitty Kat did. She leaped to me, as she always did, to be held against my shoulder. I dropped the cane, snuggled her against me. I felt her warmth, felt her chest move with her purrs, felt her breath on my cheek.

If I am dead, and can feel some things, what do I want to take with me throughout eternity? Something I love, something that gives comfort and warmth.

Kitty Kat wrapped her front legs around my neck and we left together.